LEO ROSTEN

# THE EDUCATION OF
# OF
# H★Y★M★A★N
# K★A★P★L★A★N

PENGUIN BOOKS

To "Mr. Parkhill"
after so many Waterloos

PENGUIN BOOKS

Published by the Penguin Group
27 Wrights Lane, London W8 5TZ, England
Viking Penguin Inc., 40 West 23rd Street, New York, New York 10010, USA
Penguin Books Australia Ltd, Ringwood, Victoria, Australia
Penguin Books Canada Ltd, 2801 John Street, Markham, Ontario, Canada L3R 1B4
Penguin Books (NZ) Ltd, 182–190 Wairau Road, Auckland 10, New Zealand

Penguin Books Ltd, Registered Offices: Harmondsworth, Middlesex, England

First published 1937
Published in Penguin Books 1970
This revised edition first published in Great Britain,
in a volume entitled *O K\*A\*P\*L\*A\*N! My K\*A\*P\*L\*A\*N!*,
by Constable & Co. 1979
Published in Penguin Books 1988
1 3 5 7 9 10 8 6 4 2

Made and printed in Great Britain by
Richard Clay Ltd, Bungay, Suffolk

# CONTENTS

# WARNING

The God-fearing characters in these tales do not portray persons living, dormant or dead.

Readers who insist that Miss Mitnick or Mr. Hruska, Olga Tarnova or Casimir Scymczak, act exactly like the neighbor upstairs are hallucinating: The people in these stories *do* live upstairs, but only in the house of my imagination.

L. R.

# 1

## THE RATHER BAFFLING CASE
## OF H·Y·M·A·N  K·A·P·L·A·N

"Mr. Aaron Blattberg."

"Here."

"Miss Carmen Caravello."

"Ina place!"

"Mr. Karl Finsterwald."

"Ratty!"

"Mrs. R. R. Rodriguez."

*"Sí."*

"Mr. Wolfgang Schmitt."

*"Ja!"*

"Yussel Spitz."

No answer.

"Yussel Spitz?" Mr. Parkhill looked up.

There was no Yussel Spitz.

A growl from Mr. Gus Matsoukas, in the back of the room, preceded the announcement: "He laft class. Gave op. Won't come back. He told me to say."

Mr. Parkhill made a note on his attendance sheet. He was not especially sorry, in all honesty, that Mr. Spitz had given up the ghost of learning. Mr. Spitz was an echoer. He had a startling need to repeat every question directed at him. If asked, "What is the plural of 'child'?" Mr. Spitz was sure to echo, "What is the plural of *'child'*?"—and offered no answer whatsoever. Even worse, Mr. Spitz had so spa-

3

cious a temperament that he often repeated questions asked of students two rows in front of him. This upset them. Many members of the beginners' grade had grumbled that their answers had been positively "crippled" by Yussel Spitz's prior requestioning.

"Mrs. Slavko Tomasic."

"Mm."

"Olga Tarnova."

*"Da, da."*

Besides, Mr. Parkhill thought, it was not unusual for a pupil to drop out of the American Night Preparatory School for Adults. Students came; students went. Some stayed in Mr. Parkhill's class for more than one semester; some left after only one session, or a week's, or a month's. Some enrolled because a father or mother, mate or loved one, had come to Manhattan or Brooklyn or the Bronx. Some departed because a husband's work or a wife's family drew them to another borough or another city. (Last year, a Mrs. Ingeborg Hutschner had disappeared after six weeks of conscientious attendance and commendable progress in both spelling and pronunciation; no one knew where on earth Mrs. Hutschner had gone, or why, or if she still bit her nails.)

"Miss Mitnick."

"Yes, sir," came the soft, shy voice.

And Mr. Parkhill always bore in mind that many of his students entered the portals of the A.N.P.S.A. because of the world's political upheavals: a revolution in Greece, a drought in Italy, a crisis in Germany or Cuba, a pogrom in Poland or a purge in Prague—each convulsion of power on the tormented globe was reflected, however minutely, in the school's enrollment or departures. For immigrants came to the A.N.P.S.A. not only to learn the basic, perplexing ingredients of English; they came to learn the rudiments of Civics, so that they could take the municipal

4

court's examination for that priceless, magical event: admission to citizenship.

"Mrs. Moskowitz."

"Oy."

"Mr. Kaplan."

"Here is Hyman Keplen! In poisson!"

Mr. Parkhill sighed. Mr. Kaplan baffled him. Mr. Kaplan had baffled him more than any other of the thirty-odd members of the beginners' grade ever since the very first class assignment: "Twenty Nouns and Their Plural Forms." After correcting a dozen papers, in his apartment, Mr. Parkhill came to one from which glared:

| _Nuns_ | | _Pl._ |
|--------|-------|---------------|
| house | makes | houses |
| dog | " | dogies |
| libary | " | Public libary |
| cat | " | Katz |

Mr. Parkhill had read this over several times. Then he put the page aside and tried to sort out his thoughts. He recalled Plaut and Samish's classic _Teaching English to Foreigners,_ which again and again warned teachers not to jump to the conclusion that a student was backward, a laggard or "resistant learner," before probing to the core of whatever it was that might be _causing_ the neophyte's errors. Sometimes, for instance, a slow reader needed stronger glasses, not stricter tutelage. Sometimes a poor speller was lazy, not stupid. (Spelling had nothing to do with intelligence, as the historic research of Dr. Tyler B. Ponsonby had proved.) And sometimes a pupil's errors resulted not from ignorance but from confusing _sounds:_ Mr. Parkhill had noticed that some of his students said "chicken" when they meant "kitchen," and "kitchen" when they meant "chicken." The results were mystifying. He had returned to the page before him:

5

| ear | makes | hear |
| up | " | levator |
| pan | " | pants |

Mr. Parkhill cleared his throat. All doubt now vanished: here, clearly, was a student who, if not given prompt first-aid, might easily turn into a "problem case." Anyone who believed that the plural of "cat" is "Katz" certainly needed special attention. As for transforming nouns into nuns . . .

Mr. Parkhill had run his eye down that unforgettable page, looking for the pupil's name. There was none. That was strange: the other members of the class always wrote their names at the top of the page. But no name was inscribed on the top of this page—not in the middle or at the left- or right-hand corner.

Mr. Parkhill turned the sheet over. The name was there, all right. It was printed, not written, and in large, bold letters. They looked especially bold because each character was executed in red crayon—and outlined in blue; and between every two letters sparkled a star, carefully drawn, in green. The ensemble, as triumphant as a display of fireworks, proclaimed:

H*Y*M*A*N  K*A*P*L*A*N

At the next session of the class, Mr. Parkhill had studied Mr. Kaplan with special interest. He was a plump, apple-cheeked gentleman with blondish hair and merry blue eyes, who always had *two* fountain pens clipped to the breast pocket of his jacket. (Other male pupils advertised their literacy with one.) But it was not these features that most vividly seized Mr. Parkhill's mind. It was Mr. Kaplan's smile—a bland, bright, rather charitable smile. That smile rarely left Mr. Kaplan's face. He beamed even while being corrected for the most dreadful errors in speech or spelling or grammar. He seemed to take pride in both the novelty and the number of his mistakes.

Mr. Parkhill recalled the time, in Vocabulary Building, when he had been calling off new words to the class, words to be used in oral sentences.

To "duty," Mr. Pinsky had responded: "To be a good American, please do all your duty!"

Given "nickname" (a word the pupils greeted with delight), Miss Kipnis had replied: "My name is Clara, but friends are calling me 'Cookie.' "

But presented with "choose," Mr. Kaplan had beamed: "I hate to put on a pair vet choose."

And another time, in a brisk drill on opposites, with Miss Mitnick eliciting admiration for the list she daintily wrote on the blackboard:

| | |
|------|-------|
| pull | push |
| cry | laugh |
| fix | brake |

and Wolfgang Schmitt winning hosannas for his forceful

| | |
|----------|-----------|
| work | rest |
| right | rong |
| sunshine | moonshine |

Mr. Kaplan had stunned Mr. Parkhill with

| | |
|--------|-----------|
| milk | cream |
| life | debt |
| dismay | next June |

Why, in one composition drill Mr. Kaplan had described how much he hated violins. It had taken Mr. Parkhill several damp moments to hit upon the fact that when Mr. Kaplan wrote "violins" what he probably had in mind was "violence."

Any lingering doubts about Mr. Kaplan's singular use of

7

English were resolved when he was asked to conjugate the verb "to die." Without a second's reflection, Mr. Kaplan had answered: "Die, dead, funeral."

Mr. Parkhill felt a pang of guilt. He had clearly been remiss; he had not applied himself as diligently as he should have to the case of Hyman Kaplan.

Having completed the roll call, Mr. Parkhill opened the session by announcing, "Tonight, class, let us devote ourselves to—Recitation and Speech."

A symphony of approval, punctuated by moans of dismay and groans of alarm, ascended from the rows before him. Most students enjoyed Recitation and Speech, but those who had moaned preferred writing to speaking (like Miss Valuskas, who came from Finland), and those who had groaned considered public performance of any sort out-and-out torture (like Casimir Scymczak, a plasterer from Danzig).

"Suppose we begin with Mr."—Mr. Parkhill tried to sound as if the choice was entirely spontaneous—"Kaplan."

The cherub seated in the chair he always occupied in the exact center of the front row gasped, *"Me?!"*

"Yes," smiled Mr. Parkhill. "Won't you start us off?"

"Gledly!"

"Good," said Mr. Parkhill.

"You valcome," said Mr. Kaplan.

He rose, ecstatic, stumbled over the outstretched legs of Mr. Perez (who uttered an Iberian oath), bumped the knee of Mrs. Yanoff (who hissed, "Mister, you are a fireman?!"), apologized to both colleagues with a debonair "Oxcuse," and hurried to the front of the room. Mr. Parkhill ambled to the back. (He always took a seat in the rear during Recitation and Speech.)

At Mr. Parkhill's desk, Mr. Kaplan turned to face his

8

peers. He placed one hand on the dictionary, as if posing for a statue, raised the other like a Roman reviewing his legions, broke into the sunniest of smiles, and in a ringing tenor declaimed: "Mr. Pockheel, ladies an' gantlemen, fallow mambers of beginnis' grate! For mine sobject I vill tell abot fife Prazidents fromm vunderful U.S.A. Foist, Judge Vashington, de fodder of his contry. Naxt, James Medicine, a *fine* lidder. Den, Ted E. Roosevelt, who made de Spenish Var a soccess. Also, Voodenrow Vilson, he made de voild safe for democrats. An' lest, mine *favorite* prazident, a *great* human bean, a man mit de hot an' soul of an angel: Abram Lincohen! . . . Denk you."

Mr. Kaplan strode back to his chair like a hero.

"That's a *speech?*" protested Mr. Bloom.

"Go-o-o-d-bye English," mourned Olga Tarnova.

"Oy!" That was Mrs. Moskowitz.

Mr. Parkhill cleared his throat. "That—uh—was very good, Mr. Kaplan—in content. But I'm afraid you made a con*side*rable number of mistakes in pronunciation."

"My!" chortled Mr. Kaplan.

"The floor is open for corrections," called Mr. Parkhill. "Anyone?"

The repairs came from everyone.

"I'm *dizzy* from so many mixed-op woids!" announced Aaron Blattberg.

"He pronounces 'v' like 'w'—and 'w' like 'v'!" proclaimed Mr. Marcus.

Miss Rochelle Goldberg advised Mr. Kaplan to monitor his sibilants with greater vigilance, "because you told us, teacher, how it is important to keep the difference between 's's and 'z's, so a 'ssss' shouldn't toin into a 'zzz,' and a 'zzz' —God fabid—into a 'sss'!"

Several of Miss Goldberg's cronies broke into applause. This caused Wolfgang Schmitt, who was sensitive about his own sibilants, to exclaim that "beans" are not human, and that the "ham" in President Lincoln's first name had been totally omitted. " 'Abram Lincohen' iss not Abra*ham* Lincollen!" was how Mr. Schmitt put it.

"Right!" boomed Mr. Bloom, his bald head gleaming.

"Bravo!" cried Miss Caravello.

"Class . . . please. . . ." Mr. Parkhill saw a tiny hand flutter in the air. "Miss Mitnick."

Miss Mitnick, by all odds the best student in the class, shyly observed, "The speaker can improve in his speaking, I think, if he maybe *listens* to the sounds he is making. Then he will say 'l*ea*der,' not 'l*i*dder,' also 'heart' not 'hot,' and *'fath*er,' which is absolutely different than *'fodd*er'— which is for horses, not humans."

Mr. Parkhill ignored the guffaw from Mrs. Tomasic and the cackle from Miss Gidwitz. "I agree with Miss Mitnick, Mr. Kaplan. You can greatly improve your *pro*nunciation by being careful about your *e*nunciation. For instance, we say 'f*e*llow students,' Mr. Kaplan, not 'f*a*llow students.' We say 'pr*e*sident,' not 'pr*a*zident,' and 'first,' not—er—'f*oi*st,' which is a wholly different word. And it's *'George'* Washington, Mr. Kaplan, not *'Judge'* Washington. Why, right there is a perfect example of why pronunciation is so important! Washington was a *general,* not a judge." (The news came as a blow to Mr. Kaplan.) "And if we pronounce it 'M*a*dison,' Mr. Kaplan, we are uttering the name of a President; but if you say, as you did—er—'M*e*dicine,' you are not pronouncing the name of a President, but something we take when we are sick."

The laughter (and Aaron Blattberg's scathing observation that James Madison never owned a drugstore) caused Mr. Parkhill to call on the next student at once.

What most troubled Mr. Parkhill was the fact that throughout the entire barrage of corrections from his colleagues, Mr. Kaplan smiled and chuckled and nodded his head in undisguised admiration. One could not tell whether he was congratulating his colleagues on their proficiency or preening himself on having hatched so many fascinating contributions to the English language. Mr. Parkhill felt distinctly uneasy.

During the weeks that followed, Mr. Kaplan's English showed no improvement. If anything, his mistakes increased in scope and were magnified by his enthusiasm. What made Mr. Parkhill's task doubly difficult was the fact that Mr. Kaplan was such a *willing* student. He adored learning. He never came to school late. He always worked hard. He knit his brows regularly, unfailingly submitted his homework on time, and never, never missed a class.

One evening it occurred to Mr. Parkhill that Mr. Kaplan might improve if he simply was encouraged to be a little less *hasty* in the answers he volunteered with such gusto. That insight was born during a lesson on parts of speech, when Mr. Parkhill asked Mr. Kaplan to "give a noun."

"Door," said Mr. Kaplan.

Mr. Parkhill remarked that "door" certainly was a noun, but had been supplied only a moment earlier, by Miss Ziev. "Can you give us another noun?"

"Another door," said Mr. Kaplan.

No, Mr. Kaplan could not be said to be making progress. Asked to name the opposite of "new," he had replied, "Second-hand." Told to construct a sentence using the word "fright" (which Mr. Parkhill *very* carefully enunciated), Mr. Kaplan responded: "I like fright potatoes more than smashed potatoes." And in an exercise on proper nouns, after the other students simply recited names (Lexington Avenue, Puerto Rico, New "Joisey"), Mr. Kaplan proudly announced, "Ohio!"

"Very good!"

It would have been better had not Mr. Kaplan added, "It sonds like an Indian yawnink."

An Indian yawning . . . the outlandish image haunted

11

Mr. Parkhill as he tossed and turned in his bed half that night.

Or take the pleasant, moon-bright evening Mr. Parkhill was running through a useful list of synonyms and antonyms: "Cheerful . . . Sad. Easy . . . Difficult. Lazy—"

"Kachoo!" sneezed Mrs. Shimmelfarb.

"God blast you," said Mr. Kaplan.

"*Mis*ter Kaplan," gasped Mr. Parkhill. "The expression is 'God *bless* you.' Why, you have confused 'bless' "—he printed BLESS on the board—"with 'blast' " and he printed BLAST right underneath. "The words, though somewhat similar in sound, are *entirely* different in meaning . . . I'm sure you all know what 'bless' means?"

"Sure!"

"Soitinly."

But the sage in the front row, scornful of lazy affirmations, gazed at the ceiling and murmured, " 'Bless' . . . 'Bl*ess*'?" His ruminations were audible in the back row. "Aha!" He beamed upon Mr. Parkhill: " 'Bless'! Dat's an okay fromm God."

Mr. Parkhill straightened his tie. "Y-yes . . . Now, what is the meaning of 'blast'?"

"Past tanse of 'blass'?"

"Oh, no, Mr. Kaplan. Goodness, no! The whole *point* lies in the difference between the short 'e' "—Mr. Parkhill placed the pointer on BLESS—"and the open 'a'!" He slid the pointer down to BLAST. "Who can tell us what this word means?"

"Is 'blast' a relation to gas?" asked Mr. Finsterwald.

"Well—er—gas can set off a blast. So can dynamite, or gasoline. But—"

"I think 'blast' is a type exploding," ventured Miss Mitnick.

"Precisely! *Very* good, Miss Mitnick. A blast *is*, in fact, an explosion."

"Blast gas," Mr. Kaplan decreed, searing Miss Mitnick with a superior glance.

Hard though he tried, Mr. Parkhill could discover no consistent pattern to Mr. Kaplan's many errors. They erupted in totally unpredictable ways and wholly spontaneous improvisations.

Take the evening the class was working on "a one-paragraph composition." Mr. Kaplan submitted the following:

> When two people are meating on the street [Mr. Parkhill noted that although Mr. Kaplan wrote "street" correctly, he always pronounced it "stritt"] on going Goodby, one is saying, "I am glad I mat you," but the other is giving answer, "Mutchual."

It had taken twelve minutes for the class to complete its autopsy on that one paragraph.

But it was in Recitation and Speech, which elicited Mr. Kaplan's greatest affection, that that intrepid scholar soared to new and unnerving heights. One night, carried away by his eloquence, Mr. Kaplan referred to America's first First Lady as "Mother Washington." Mr. Parkhill was compelled to employ all his powers of persuasion before he could convince Mr. Kaplan that although George Washington was the father of his country, that did not make Martha the *mother*.

Or take the time Mr. Kaplan followed young Vincente Perez's eulogy to Cervantes, whom he proclaimed the greatest writer "een all the world litterture." Mr. Kaplan cast a scornful eye upon Mr. Perez as he delivered a patriotic rejoinder: "Greatest authors are from U.S." The greatest and most "beauriful" American authors (he had read them, it seemed, in his native tongue) were "Jek Laundon, Valt Vitterman, an' de creator of two vunderful books for grown pipple an' boyiss: 'Hawk L. Barryfeen' an' 'Toms Oyer.'"

Mr. Kaplan explained that he was not conferring laurel wreaths on "Edgar Allen Pope" because that wizard had written mysteries, a genre Mr. Kaplan did not admire, nor on "Hoiman Malville," because "Mopy Dick gives more attantion to fish dan to pipple."

The whole episode had so alarmed Mr. Parkhill that he asked Mr. Kaplan to remain after class, to discuss his disastrous reversals of the open "a" and the short "e" ("A *pat*, Mr. Kaplan, is not a *pet;* nor is a pet a pat!"); his repeated transpositioning of the short "i" and the long "e" (Mr. Kaplan once advised the class to patronize only those dentists who are so skillful that they can "feel a cavity so you don't iven fill it"); his deplorable propensity for converting the hard "g" into the startling "k," and the broad "o" into the short "u" (Mr. Kaplan transformed "dogs" into "dugs," and "sucks" into "socks").

To all these earnest supplications, Mr. Kaplan responded with ardent thanks, abject guilt, and an exuberant promise to "chenge vunce an' for all all mine bed hebits!"

Plaut and Samish contained not one page about a student who wedded such willingness to such unteachability.

Everything, Mr. Parkhill feared, pointed to the likelihood that Mr. Kaplan would have to remain in the beginners' grade for an extra year. How could such a pupil possibly be promoted to Miss Higby's Advanced Grammar and Civics? The fear was strengthened in Mr. Parkhill's mind the night Mrs. Yanoff read a sentence from the textbook *English for Beginners* about the "vast deserts of Arizona." (Mrs. Yanoff, a lugubrious pupil, always wore black, though Mr. Yanoff was far from dead.) In the discussion that followed, Mr. Parkhill learned that Mrs. Yanoff did not understand the meaning of "vast"; she thought it a misprint for "best."

So Mr. Parkhill turned to the blackboard and there

printed VAST. "Well, class," he smiled, "who can tell us the meaning of 'vast'?"

Up shot Mr. Kaplan's hand.

"Yes?"

"Ve have four diractions: naut, sot, yeast, an' vast."

"No, no. That is *'west,'* Mr. Kaplan." On the board he printed WEST under VAST. "There is a *considerable* difference in meaning between these two words—apart from the fact that the first is pronounced *'v-v-v*ast,' Mr. Kaplan, and the second *'w-w-w*est.' "

This seemed to flash a new light into Mr. Kaplan's inner world. "Aha! So de void you eskink abot is *'v-v*ast' an' not *'w-w*ast.' "

" 'W*est*,' " said Mr. Parkhill, "not 'w*a*st.' You *must* watch those 'e's and 'a's!"

"Hau Kay. De void you esk is not 'w*e*st' but 'v*a*st'?"

Mr. Parkhill declared that "vast" was indeed the *"word"* for which he was *"ask*ing."

"So—" Mr. Kaplan beamed. "Ven a man buys a suit, he gats de cawt, de pents, an' de vast."

Mr. Parkhill lowered his chalk. "I—uh—am afraid you have introduced still another word."

Mr. Kaplan awaited the plaudits of the crowd.

" 'V*e*st,' " frowned Mr. Parkhill, "is an article of clothing, but 'west' . . ."

And then Mr. Kaplan turned Mr. Parkhill's concern into consternation. It came during Open Questions. Open Questions was Mr. Parkhill's own invention, a half-session devoted to answering any questions his students might care to raise about any difficulties with English they might have encountered in the course of their daily work and life. The beginners' grade loved Open Questions. So did Mr. Parkhill. He enjoyed helping his flock with practical problems; he felt ever so much more constructive that way. (Miss Higby often told Miss Schnepfe, secretary to the principal of the A.N.P.S.A., that if ever there was a born Open Questions teacher it was Mr. Parkhill.)

"Questions, anyone? *Any* questions—spelling, grammar, pronun—"

Gus Matsoukas emitted his introductory growl, consulted a dog-eared envelope, and muttered his question. "For furniture: is it 'baboon' or *bam*boon'?"

"Well, a 'baboon' is a type of—er—ape," said Mr. Parkhill, "whereas 'bamboo' is a certain wood. Bamboo is what is used in furniture. *Baboons* are—er—what you may see in a zoo. . . . Next?"

"The word 'stamp'—for putting on mail. Isn't that masculine?" asked Bessie Shimmelfarb.

"N-no," said Mr. Parkhill, and stressed the difference between the postal and the human. (Mrs. Shimmelfarb had obviously equated "mail" with "male.") "Next question?"

"What is the League of Women Motors?" Miss Gidwitz, a fervent feminist, inquired.

"The League of Women *Voters,*" said Mr. Parkhill, "is an organization . . ." His exposition led several women to applaud.

"Who was Madame Pumpernickel?" asked Oscar Trabish, who was a baker. (Mr. Trabish's occupation often affected his diction.)

"Madame *Pompadour,*" gulped Mr. Parkhill, "was a famous character in French history. She was King Louis XIV's—er—favorite. She—"

"Pompadour is a type haircut!" protested Barney Vinograd, who was a barber.

"Oh, it *is,*" agreed Mr. Parkhill at once. "The name *comes* from Madame Pompadour, who wore her hair—that way."

"Haddya like that?!" breathed Goldie Pomeranz.

"Aducation, aducation," beamed Hyman Kaplan, tendering gratitude to the wonders of learning.

" 'Merit'!" That was Mrs. Moskowitz.

"I beg your pardon?"

" 'Merit,' " Mrs. Moskowitz repeated. "Why isn't it pernonced the way it's spelt?"

Mr. Parkhill looked puzzled. "But 'merit' is spelled exactly as it is pronounced, Mrs. Moskowitz." He printed MERIT on the board. "Don't you see?"

"I see it, but I don't mean it!" Mrs. Moskowitz complained. *"That* woid I never saw in mine whole life! *I* mean, if a boy and goil are in love, they get—"

" 'Married'!" exclaimed Mr. Parkhill. "Oh, that's an entirely different word, Mrs. Moskowitz." His chalk crowned MERIT with MARRIED.

"Oy," sighed Sadie Moskowitz.

"Next question? . . . Mr. Kaplan."

Mr. Kaplan asked, "Mr. Pockheel, vhat's de minnink fromm 'A big depotment'?"

"It's 'de*part*ment,' Mr. Kaplan," said Mr. Parkhill. "Well, class, I'm sure you have all shopped in a large downtown store." A majority nodded. "Now, in these stores, if you want to buy, say, a shirt, you go to a special *part* of the store, where only shirts are sold: that is called the shirt *department."* The quorum assented. "And if you want to buy, say, a goldfish"—Plaut and Samish approved of lightening a lesson with occasional levity—"you would go to another part of the store, where—er—goldfish are for sale . . . So, you see, each article is sold, or purchased, in a different, special place. And these different, special places are called—'departments.' " Mr. Parkhill printed DEPARTMENT on the blackboard. "Therefore, a *big* department, Mr. Kaplan, is merely a department which is large—big." He put the chalk down. "Is that clear, class?"

It was perfectly clear to the class—except, apparently,

Mr. Kaplan, who was blinking blankly.

"Isn't my explanation clear, Mr. Kaplan?" asked Mr. Parkhill anxiously.

"Ebsolutely! It's a *fine* axplination, Mr. Pockheel. Clear like soda-vater. Foist-class! *A* number vun! . . . But I don't unnistand vhy I hear dat void in de *vay* I do. Simms to me, it's used in anodder *minnink.*"

"There's really only one meaning for 'department.' "

"Maybe it's not 'a' big depotment but *'I* big depotment.' "

Mr. Parkhill surveyed the ceiling. " *'I* big department' does not make *sense,* Mr. Kaplan. Let me repeat my explanation." This time Mr. Parkhill enlisted the aid of a hat department, a pajama department, and "a separate part of the store where, for example, you buy—canaries, or other birds."

Mr. Kaplan hung on to Mr. Parkhill's every word; but at "canaries, or other birds," he shook his head.

"What is it that puzzles you, Mr. Kaplan?"

"Mr. Pockheel, I'm vary sorry, but I don't simm to make mine qvastion clear. So I'll give you de exect vay I hoid dat axpression . . . I'm takink a valk. In de stritt. An' I mit a frand. So I stop to say a few polite voids, like: 'Hollo,' 'Harre you?,' 'How you fill?' An' vhile ve are talkink, along comms somvun alse, pessink by, an' by exident he's givink me a bump. So he says, 'Axcuse me,' no? But *somtimes,* an' dis is vat I minn, he says, 'Oh, I big depotment!' "

For one shameless moment Mr. Parkhill wondered whether he could reconcile it with his conscience if he did promote Mr. Kaplan to Advanced Grammar and Civics. Another three months in the beginners' grade might, after all, be nothing but a waste of Mr. Kaplan's time.

# 2

## MR. K·A·P·L·A·N SLAYS {2}
## THE SUPERLATIVE

Each week, Mr. Parkhill found it harder to face up to the possibility that Mr. Kaplan might have to be kept in the beginners' grade for some time to come. Promotion to Miss Higby's Advanced Grammar and Civics, at the end of the semester, seemed quite out of the question. It was folly even to think of it. (From time to time, because the idea was so tempting, Mr. Parkhill did think of it, but it was folly to cling to it.)

Every assignment Mr. Kaplan fulfilled contained some new and startling reformation of the English language. (In his most recent composition, Mr. Kaplan had written: "Each year our President gives Congriss a personal massage.") What Mr. Parkhill had to face, without shilly-shallying, was the fact that Mr. Kaplan was no ordinary pupil. Mr. Kaplan was no ordinary man, for that matter. His thirst for knowledge clashed with his passion for originality. He seemed to confuse education with imagination. Mr. Parkhill had even begun to wonder whether Mr. Kaplan's audacious innovations did not contain the seeds of a new English grammar (to say nothing of a new diction, reformed spelling, and refreshed pronunciation). Sometimes Mr. Parkhill felt that Mr. Kaplan was the apostle of an entirely new way of *thinking*.

To Hyman Kaplan, for instance, the instrument most

often used by plumbers is a "monkey ranch," blunders in speech are caused by "a sleeping of the tong," and the opposite of "do" is "donut." How could Mr. Parkhill blind himself to the nonpromotability of such a scholar? The man was, to put it bluntly, *sui generis*.

For two nights now, Mr. Parkhill had been fending off in his mind the fact that Mr. Kaplan would have to write his composition on the blackboard. All the names on the class roll had been ticked off except Tarnova, Caravello, and Kaplan. The rest had transcribed their homework during the week drawing to its end.

The acuteness of the class discussion had been gratifying. How swiftly had Miss Mitnick deduced that in Mr. Trabish's essay, "Hannah Lou" was not the name of a laundress, but the capital of Hawaii. How unerringly had Mrs. Slavko Tomasic caught Shirley Ziev's odd revision of Genesis: "Adam and Eve lived in the Garden of Eton." And with what scorn had not Aaron Blattberg pointed out that the "Wilhelm" twice mentioned in Mr. Finsterwald's essay must refer to an "uncle—and not, as he wrote, an 'ankle'!"

Yes, those sessions had greatly heartened Mr. Parkhill. But the composition of Hyman Kaplan was yet to be seen. It would be more accurate to say that the composition of H*Y*M*A*N K*A*P*L*A*N was yet to be seen, for even in thinking of that singular student Mr. Parkhill could not help beholding that singular signature. At first, Mr. Parkhill considered the red-blue-green starred name as a sort of trademark, or a harmless expression of pride. But lately, he had come to realize it was *much* more than that: the crayoned letters were not a name but a proclamation (in his youth, Mr. Kaplan had yearned to be "a physician and sergeant"), a symbol of individuality, a declaration of independence from the chains of the conventional. Only last week, Mr. Kaplan had given the principal parts of the verb "to fail" as "fail, failed, bankrupt."

Tonight, the fateful hour had come. There was just no way to defer Mr. Kaplan's homework further, nor cling to the hope that perhaps Mr. Kaplan would leave the room early: that loyal scholar had not once been so much as a minute late, nor left one second early.

"Miss Tarnova..." Mr. Parkhill heard himself intoning. "Miss Caravello ... Mr. Kaplan ... I believe it is your turn to place your homework on the board."

Carmen Caravello gave a cheerful *"Bene!"* Olga Tarnova uttered a dolorous *"Górye."* Mr. Kaplan breathed his joyous "My!"

Miss Caravello tripped to the blackboard. Miss Tarnova trudged as if on her way to the guillotine. And Mr. Kaplan passed one full board beyond Miss Tarnova's terrain, Mr. Parkhill noticed, humming a ditty of delight. Mr. Kaplan inspected several pieces of chalk, rejected them, found a stick worthy of its task, and printed:

MINE JOB
Comp. by
H*Y*

"You need not write your *name* on the board," called Mr. Parkhill quickly.

Mr. Kaplan's face was a funnel of astonishment.

"Er—to save time," faltered Mr. Parkhill.

"I got planty time," said Mr. Kaplan.

"I meant the class's time."

Mr. Kaplan blinked. "But mine name is a dafinite *pot* of mine composition."

"Oh."

Dignity restored, Mr. Kaplan completed his starry signature. The sigh with which he invested the printing of the final "N" testified to the pain he suffered in not being allowed to use colored chalks.

As Carmen Caravello sped through her assignment, and

Olga Tarnova glowered through hers, Mr. Kaplan transferred his homework from the paper which rustled in his left hand to the slate which did not flinch from his right. As he wrote, he kept his tongue in the corner of his mouth; and he executed eloquent rotations of the elbow and periodic flourishes of the wrist. But he kept his little finger genteelly extended, an aristocratic digit for whom the other four toiled. The entire elegant process was accompanied by *sotto voce* chuckles and distinct purrings of glory.

As Miss Tarnova scrawled away, her looped earrings jingled and her gaudy bracelets jangled. Mr. Kaplan stared at the offending artifacts. "Tarnova, are you wridink homevoik or givink a concert?"

The glare Miss Tarnova shot him would have slain a Borzoi. "I am womon!" she retorted.

"You sond more like an orchestra."

"Students . . ." Mr. Parkhill cut in. "There is no need to—"

"Eider she should take off or tune op her joolery," recommended Mr. Kaplan.

*"Bodzhe moi!"* That throaty oath, like everything about Olga Tarnova—her raven hair and satin dress, her perfumed handkerchief and sultry eyes—conveyed intimations of the time she was the toast of the Monte Carlo Ballet. (More than once had Miss Tarnova hinted that there was a time when princes of the blood, maddened by her beauty, had fought duels behind the great Casino for her favors.) *"Bodzhe moi!"*

"Are ve stodyink Rossian or English?" cooed Mr. Kaplan.

"Mr. *Kap—!*"

The Slavic siren snapped her handkerchief in Mr. Kaplan's direction in silken rebuke, completed her essay, and sailed grandly back to her chair. Mr. Parkhill scanned what she had written:

I make hats. They are pretty. New shapes. All collars. Womens come from all over N.Y. to buy each other.

But millinery is not my love. It was in Ballet. Ah, Ballet, Ballet. I am sad.

O. T.

Miss Caravello completed her offering: "How Bella Bella is Roma Roma!" The celebration of Rome's beauties was not more than a hundred words long, yet managed to cram in two arches, three piazzas, and a considerable number of fountains.

Mr. Kaplan finished last, with a reluctant "Hau Kay," wiped his fingers delicately, analyzed his handiwork through narrowed eyes, nodding a benediction over his masterpiece, and returned to his chair in the stride of one preparing for coronation.

"Class, study Miss Tarnova's composition first . . ." announced Mr. Parkhill absently, for his eyes were racing across Mr. Kaplan's opus:

### MINE JOB
Comp. by
H*Y*M*A*N  K*A*P*L*A*N

Shakspere is saying what fulls Man is! And I am feeling the same when thinking about my job in Faktory on 38 st. by 7 av.

Why should we svet and slafe in a dark place by chip laktric and all kinds hot? For who? A Boss who is salfish, fat, driving a fency automibil?? I ask! I answer—because we are the deprassed workers of the world.

O how bad is that laktric light! O how is all kinds hot! And when I tell the Forman should be better work condittions— he hollers, "Kaplan you redical!!" Which I am not. I am only human, the same as you and me.

Mr. Parkhill's temples began to throb.

> So now I keep my mot shot. But somday will the Union win!! Then Kaplan will make the Forman a worker, and will give him the most bad stiles to cot ot! Justice.
>
> My job is a cotter mens cloths.

T-H-E E-N-D

"Well, class . . ." Mr. Parkhill could think of nothing else to say. "Let us begin with Miss Tarnova's composition . . . Who would like to start?"

Four hands popped into the air.

"Mr. Blattberg."

" 'Collars' is spelled bad," said Aaron Blattberg. "Should be 'c-o-l-o-r-s.' "

"Very good." Mr. Parkhill erased "collars" and inserted "colors." "Miss Kipnis?"

" 'Womens' is not a plural," Miss "Cookie" Kipnis observed, "but 'women,' spelled like 'men,' and without the 's.' "

"Correct!" Mr. Parkhill removed the terminal "s" from "womens." "The word 'women' is itself plural, so it needs no 's.' If you *do* use an 's,' it must be preceded by an apostrophe, this way"—he printed WOMEN'S—"which makes it *possessive,* not plural. For instance"—he tapped WOMEN'S with his pointer—"suppose we wanted to say 'women's hats' or 'women's rights'—"

"Or 'vimen's *mistakes,' "* Mr. Kaplan leered at Olga Tarnova.

"—then the apostrophe would be required. But an 's' after a word which is already plural is—er—superfluous."

The room hummed and buzzed over this increment to knowledge, but Rochelle Goldberg asked, "What means 'superfloss'? Is that big-size dental—"

" '*Su*perfluous!' " Mr. Parkhill exclaimed. "That means 'not needed.' It *is* a rather—advanced word. I'm sorry. I

24

should have said that an 's' after a plural noun is not *necessary. . . ."*

"Thank you." Miss Goldberg reached into her purse for a gumdrop. (Miss Goldberg liked to reward her labors with a bonbon.)

"Further comments? . . . Miss Valuskas."

Gerta Valuskas observed that contrary to Olga Tarnova's unfortunate wording, the women who came to her millinery shop did not actually "buy each other." What they did was "buy hats *for* one and the other."

The class acclaimed the Valuskas acumen: "You right!" "Absolutely!" "Good corracting!"

"Very good, Miss Valuskas. . . . Miss Tarnova, do you understand that?"

"No."

Mr. Parkhill cleared his throat.

"Well—er—just notice. You wrote 'they' (that is, women) come to your store and—'buy each *other.*' That—"

"Maybe Tarnova sells hats an' also vimen . . ."

*"Mr.* Kaplan!" Mr. Parkhill said sharply. (He could hardly permit one student to accuse another of white slavery.) "What you should have said, Miss Tarnova, is that your clientele buy hats as presents *for* each other. Now do you see?"

"Ah, da, da," moaned Olga Tarnova.

"Any other comments? Mr. Schmitt . . ."

"I sink zat Miz Tarnova should tell us more about ze *army,"* said Wolfgang Schmitt.

Mr. Parkhill hesitated. " 'Army,' Mr. Schmitt? What army?"

"Ze Rossian army."

Mr. Parkhill frowned. "But why—"

"Because she wrote—zere, on ze board—about her work in ze military—"

"No, no, no!" exclaimed Mr. Parkhill. " 'Millinery' is not

'*military*,' Mr. Schmitt!" He wrote "military" on the board swiftly.

"Schmitt batter not show his face in de gomment district," observed Mr. Kaplan.

The clock stood at 9:30; time was running out. Mr. Parkhill said, "Let us proceed to Mr. Kaplan's composition."

"Oy," prophesied Mrs. Moskowitz. (To Sadie Moskowitz "oy" was not a word; it was a lexicon.)

Mr. Kaplan said, "Is planty mistakes, I s'pose . . ."

"Y-yes, Mr. Kaplan. I'm afraid there are."

"Dat's becawss I try to give dip *ideas.*"

Mr. Parkhill pondered his inner resources. "First, class, one might say that Mr. Kaplan does not give us much description of his job—"

"It's not soch an interastink jop."

"—and wrote not a composition so much as an—er—editorial."

"I'm producink adi*to*rials?" rejoiced Mr. Kaplan.

"We must confine ourselves to simple exercises," said Mr. Parkhill sternly, "before we attempt political essays."

"So naxt time should be no *ideas?*" asked Mr. Kaplan. "Only plain fects?"

" '*F*acts,' Mr. Kaplan, not '*f*ects.' "

Mr. Kaplan's expression left no doubt that his wings, like those of an eagle, were being clipped.

"And, Mr. Kaplan, may I ask why it is that you use 'Kaplan' in the body of your composition? Why didn't you write '*I* will make the foreman a worker'? instead of '*Kaplan* will make—' "

"I didn't vant de reader should t'ink I am prajudiced. So I put de onfrandly remocks abot foremen like in de mot of a strenger."

Mr. Parkhill called for corrections.

A forest of hands, palms, pencils, pens, rulers, notebooks sprang into the air.

"Miss Mitnick."

Miss Mitnick had gathered a veritable bushel of errors —in spelling, punctuation, diction, syntax—and she recited them with rapid rectitude. "—and that *'mot shot,'*" she concluded, blushing, "should be 'm*outh*'—'*o-u*'—'shut' —'*u*' instead '*o.*' And that isn't a nice way to talk, besides!"

"Very good," said Mr. Parkhill.

"*Ax*cellent!" beamed Mr. Kaplan, baffling Miss Mitnick.

"Mr. Bloom . . ."

Norman Bloom fired a salvo at no fewer than eight errant words, six crippled sentences, nine deformed phrases, and two throttled infinitives, finishing the onslaught with "—and workers are depressed with an 'e' not an 'a'!"

"Bloom," chuckled Mr. Kaplan, "you soitinly improvink!"

"*I'm* improving?" Mr. Bloom protested, mopping his pate. "It's *your* composition we are discussing!"

"An' in discossink, you improvink!"

"This mon," mourned Miss Tarnova. "This *mon . . .*"

"Mr. Matsoukas."

Gus Matsoukas indignantly changed "fulls" to "fools," "cloths" to "clothes," and hotly challenged the propriety of "Justice" standing all by itself, unsupported, "in one-word-not-sentence!" No one dared challenge a Platonist where justice was at stake.

Then Miss Gidwitz declared, with some force, that Mr. Kaplan meant "'*opp*ressed,' not '*dep*ressed,' workers of the world!"

"Aren't day deprassed, too?" rejoined Mr. Kaplan.

"Mr. Blattberg?"

The massacre of Mr. Kaplan's essay neither flagged nor faltered. Mr. Blattberg blurted out a catalogue of acid rectifications. Mrs. Tomasic tendered a poisoned bouquet of praise: "Mr. Keplen has a big imagination, but look how he spelled wrong Shakespeare's name!" Even Casimir

Scymczak leaped into the melee, belying the complexity of his name by the simplicity of his attack: "Why Mr. Koplen writes 'chip'? Is 'c-h-e-a-p.' Why letters *'t-o'* when is *'t-o-o'* for 'also.' "

"Bravo!" gloated Miss Caravello.

And when the heated scholars had exhausted both their knowledge and their umbrage, Mr. Parkhill took over. It was astonishing how many blunders Mr. Kaplan could commit in such limited space. Mr. Parkhill altered tenses, added commas, removed periods; he changed the indirect to the direct (and the direct to the indirect) object; he pointed out that it was wrong to say "I am only human, the same as you and me" because the "I am" clearly made the "and me" redundant.

Throughout the whole fusillade, Hyman Kaplan sank into neither passivity nor despond; instead, he sighed, coughed, chuckled, closed his eyes, held his forehead, clucked his tongue, exclaimed "My!" or "Tchk-tchk!" or "Haddaya like dat?" at strategic intervals. The forehead-holding showed amazement, the cough was pure demurrer, the tongue-clucking implied self-blame, but the expletives tendered consolation to his ego.

"Finally, class, let me call your attention to an error—a very *important* error—which no one has noticed." Mr. Parkhill ran his pointer along the line which described the fate that awaited Mr. Kaplan's foreman should that heartless tyrant ever be replaced by Mr. Kaplan himself:

. . . and will give him the most bad stiles to cot ot!

"Please notice 'most bad stiles.' (That should be a *'y,'* incidentally, not an 'i.') 'Most bad,' class, is totally incorrect! There *is* a word, a common word, for 'most bad,' just as there is for the 'most' of other adjectives. It is the form called—the superlative. . . ."

"Oy," wailed Mrs. Moskowitz.

"We need not be frightened by the word 'superlative,'" said Mr. Parkhill earnestly. "We just use different adjectives—really, different forms of the same adjective—whenever we want to describe something, then want to *compare* it to another thing, and then if we want to show that it is even more so than all the other things to which we may wish to compare it!"

A new *"Oy-y-y"* indicated that Mrs. Moskowitz was not frightened but horrified.

"Notice how *simple* it is!" exclaimed Mr. Parkhill. "For example, we say that someone or something is 'tall.' . . ." He printed TALL more swiftly than he had ever printed anything on the board before. "This is the first or 'positive' form. Now, if we want to say that someone—let's call him John—is 'tall*er*' than, say, his sister"—a quickly chalked TALLER overshadowed TALL—"that is the 'comparative' form. And when we want to say that John is taller than everyone in the family, or any other group—I mean whenever we compare *more than two* persons or objects or even ideas—we say 'tall*est*'!". TALLEST promptly towered over its siblings. "And *that* form, using 'e-s-t,' is called—the 'superlative'! Do you see?"

"I *see!*" blushed Miss Mitnick.

"Yos," said Mr. Scymczak.

"My!" glowed Mr. Kaplan.

Miss Goldberg swallowed a marshmallow.

"Now, class, let us see how easy it is with other adjectives. Take—oh—'rich.' 'Rich . . . rich*er* . . . rich*est* . . .'" He paraded the wealthy trio down the board. "Or—'strong'! . . . 'Strong . . . strong*er* . . . strong*est.*'"

Rapture swept the forum; ejaculations of joy hailed the miracle of education.

"Now, isn't that easy, class?"

"Easy!" echoed Mrs. Yanoff, who rarely found anything easy.

"A snep!" grinned Sam Pinsky.

"You *mov*velous!" cheered Mr. Kaplan.

Mr. Parkhill was so pleased by their enthusiasm that he permitted himself a modest smile. "Let us see how many other examples *you* can volunteer."

"Sick, sicker, sickest," sang out Miss Mitnick.

"Good!"

"Dark, darker, darkest," offered Mr. Feigenbaum.

*"Very* good."

"Da fat, da fatter, da fa-a-atest!" trilled Carmen Caravello.

"Excellent. . . . And now, class, let me take one moment to note that there are certain exceptions—"

Groans instantly greeted the ominous "exceptions." The beginners' grade had long ago learned to fear—nay, loathe —the Exception to the Rule. It was the bane of their learning, a snake in the garden of perception. (Mr. Krout, the senior instructor in the A.N.P.S.A., once enlivened a faculty meeting by declaring that "the very *bête noir* of English is the skulking multitude of Exceptions to the Rule!" How Mr. Parkhill had admired the way Mr. Krout had put that! He admired it almost as much as he admired Mr. Robinson, the school principal, for responding: "I heartily agree, Mr. Krout. There are as many exceptions to the rule in English as there were thieves in Baghdad!" Who could forget such a simile? "But we cannot *change* the rules of grammar—nor, if I may say so, can we exile all the exceptions. . . . Carry on! That is what we all must do. Carry on!" If there was one quality Mr. Parkhill had inherited from his ancestors, it was the capacity to carry on.)

"Class," said Mr. Parkhill, "it is not as complicated as you assume. For instance, take the adjective 'good.' We don't say 'good . . . gooder . . . goodest . . .,' do we?"

"Oh, *no,*" said Miss Mitnick.

"Never!" called adamant Bloom.

30

"It's to leff!" laughed Mr. Kaplan.

"Quite so. 'Good, gooder, goodest' is ridiculous. . . . What do we say, then? 'X' is good, 'Y' is—"

"Who," demanded Mrs. Moskowitz, "is dis 'X'?"

" 'X' is just a symbol," said Mr. Parkhill, "a *sign* for, well, any name or thing. . . . So, we say 'X' is good, but 'Y' is—"

"Who is *'Y'*?"

"Anodder tsymbol!" snapped Mr. Kaplan. "Fa goodness *sek,* Moskovitz, don't you onnistand a *semple,* a plain 'for instance'?"

"My had is swimming," moaned Mrs. Moskowitz.

"Your had is *dron*ink," said Mr. Kaplan. "Lat Mr. Pockheel halp you ot—"

" '*H*e*lp you *out,'* Mr. Kaplan!" Mr. Parkhill's pointer tapped the desk with resolution. "Again, please. We say that something is 'good,' " he raised his voice, "and that something is even—" He arched an eyebrow.

"Batter," yawned Mr. Trabish, ever the baker.

"Exactly! And for our *utmost* praise, when something is superior to even that which is better, we say—?"

"High-cless!"

Mr. Parkhill's pointer froze in midair. "Oh, no, Mr. Kaplan."

*"Not* 'high-cless'?" Mr. Kaplan could not believe his ears.

"No, Mr. Kaplan. The word is 'best.' . . . And now, to return to your phrase, 'most bad.' What is the comparative form of 'bad'? . . . Anyone? 'Bad' . . ."

"Worse," volunteered Goldie Pomeranz.

"Correct! And the superlative?"

"Also 'worse'?"

"N-no, Miss Pomeranz—although the superlative certainly sounds a *great* deal like 'worse.' You are *very* close . . . I'm sure you know the answer. 'X' is 'bad,' 'Y' is 'worse,' and 'Z' is—?"

"Now comes Mr. 'Z'?!" Mrs. Moskowitz's incredulity broke all bounds.

" 'Bad . . . worse . . .' and—?"

"Aha!" cried Mr. Kaplan. "I got it!"

"Good."

"De exect void!"

"Go on."

" 'Rotten!' "

The pointer fell out of Mr. Parkhill's hand. He bent down to pick it up, thoughtfully placed it on its ledge, fumbled for a stick of chalk, and printed W-O-R-S-T on the battle-scarred slate.

And all the while he was executing these movements, Mr. Parkhill's mind churned with this latest manifestation of Mr. Kaplan's exasperating originality: "Bad . . . worse . . . rotten. Bad . . . worse . . ."

The bell tolled reprieve down the corridor. What cared that mindless gong that Miss Caravello's "Bella, Bella, Roma, Roma" still glared, unhonored and uncriticized, on the board?

# 3

## O HEARTLESS HOMONYMS!

Ever since Mrs. Yanoff had made the extraordinary error of endowing Mary's little lamb with "fleas as white as snow," Mr. Parkhill realized that the beginners' grade was in dire need of a lesson on homonyms. Strictly speaking, "fleas" and "fleece" were not homonyms, since the words are spelled differently, not alike (as, say, "bow . . . bow," the first meaning to bend, the second linked to an arrow). "Fleas" and "fleece" are not even homophones: that is, words spelled differently but pronounced alike (as, say, "bear . . . bare").

But whatever the technical jargon (and Mr. Parkhill was extremely careful not to confuse his students with grue-some words such as homonym or homophone), there was no doubt in his mind that a lesson on words spelled alike but pronounced differently, or words spelled differently but pronounced alike, would be extremely useful.

During the next sessions of his class, Mr. Parkhill kept on the alert for some student's misuse of either a homo-nym or a homophone. His opportunity came when Miss Pomeranz, in an otherwise commendable composition, wrote:

He pulled off a piece of the tree's bark.

Mr. Matsoukas promptly growled, "Trees are not dogs! *Dogs* bark."

33

"Zo what do treess do, zing?" demanded Wolfgang Schmitt.

"Don't be silly," yawned Mr. Trabish. "Trees are daf an' dump."

"One moment!" Mr. Parkhill broke in. "A *very* interesting point is involved here. Miss Pomeranz used a word which has two different meanings—in fact as Mr. Matsoukas's comment tells us, 'bark' is really *two* different words, spelled exactly alike!"

Astonishment swept the synod, some of whom had never credited Miss Pomeranz with such virtuosity, and some of whom were stunned by yet another revelation of the duplicity of the English tongue.

"Two words spelled one way?" moaned Olga Tarnova.

"Loin, Tarnova, don't complain!" snapped Mr. Kaplan. "In ballet didn't you dance a dance?!"

"Precisely!" Mr. Parkhill stepped to the blackboard. "Notice, class." He printed:

BARK
BARK

"The spellings are identical. But the first 'bark' means the covering of a tree or a branch—"

"Aha!"

"—whereas the second is the sound made by a dog."

"Bow-wow!" came from Mr. Matsoukas.

"Now it's a school for *animals?!*" wailed Miss Ziev.

"Class," called Mr. Parkhill cheerfully, "I think you will all be greatly interested if we devote the rest of the session to just such words!"

"I'm already eenterested," vowed Mrs. Rodriguez.

"Goot idea!" declared Mr. Pinsky.

Mr. Schmitt called, "Zat could be ze most zuccezzful lezzon zis zemester—"

"I hear *bees* in de room," observed Mr. Kaplan.

"Mr. Kaplan! That was not necessary," frowned Mr. Parkhill.

"If Schmitt said 'necessary' it vould sond like a stimm-cattle!"

"'Steam,' not 'stimm,'" said Mr. Parkhill severely. "And—"

"'Cattle' for 'kettle'?!" Mr. Bloom guffawed. "Kaplan, do you boil water on a cow?!"

Laughter shook the ranks. Miss Tarnova waved her handkerchief. Mr. Blattberg was in ecstasy. How Mr. Kaplan felt, no one could tell. Whenever Mr. Kaplan was driven against a wall which neither ingenuity nor guile could surmount, he simply reasserted his dignity, arranging his features into disdain for the rabble whose indignities were beneath response from a man of honor.

"Class . . . class . . ." Mr. Parkhill's pointer finally stilled the commotion. "Please give me your full attention. I said that some words, such as 'bark,' look exactly alike and are pronounced exactly alike, but have wholly different meanings. Now, other words are spelled alike but are *pronounced* differently—" In a flash he printed:

1. COMBINE
2. COMBINE

"The first means to put together—'com*bine*,' but the second, '*com*-bine,' is an organized group—"

"How can I tell the difference?!" rasped Jacob Marcus.

"By the context," said Mr. Parkhill earnestly. "I mean the whole sentence in which the word is used. It's only a matter of becoming familiar—"

"I'll *never* be familiar!" predicted Miss Kipnis.

"Of course you will," said Mr. Parkhill. "We *all* have had to learn such—things. . . . And then there is a third group of words, spelled alike, and pronounced alike, but—"

"What?!" cried Bessie Shimmelfarb.

"Ooooo." Mrs. Moskowitz was trying to sound genteel.

"—totally different in meaning!"

"Oy!" came the diphthong of total despair.

"It's *extremely* interesting," said Mr. Parkhill quickly, and just as quickly plied chalk on board:

1. FAST
2. FAST

"Now, class, you see that both 'fasts' are spelled exactly alike. And both are *pronounced* alike. Yet"—he paused, aware that some minds would reel, much confidence crash with his words—"the *meaning* of 'Fast' Number One is entirely different from the meaning of 'Fast' Number Two, and vice ver—"

Not a crash but an earthquake shook the walls. The cries of disbelief, the howls of protest, the outraged accusations of trickery—the room rang with the piteous gabble of victims fleeing for their lives.

" 'Fast' Number One," called Mr. Parkhill above the uproar, "is wholly unlike 'Fast' Number Two because . . ."

"No!"

*"Hanh?!"*

Rochelle Goldberg was gobbling raisins as if they were penicillin.

*"Please* listen." Mr. Parkhill tapped the first "fast" with his pointer. "This means 'quick' or 'speedy,' and *this*"—he rattled the stick at the second and confounding "fast"— "means not to eat!"

Light struck Mr. Pinsky. "Like on Yom Kippur!"

"Right!" said Mr. Parkhill. "Now, note *this* pair." His winged chalk flew across the center of the board:

1. INTEREST
2. INTEREST

"The first 'interest' means to engage our attention or curiosity—"

"You—interesta—us!" sang Miss Caravello.

"Thank you. But the *second* 'interest' is what you receive for putting money in a savings bank."

"I dun't be*lieve* it!" said Mr. Feigenbaum.

"I do," sneered Mr. Kaplan.

"A bank isn't interested in interest?" bleated Mr. Wilkomirski, who often mixed things up badly.

"But how do we know if the word means interesting or a profit?" Mr. Blattberg twirled his watch chain, from which the baby tooth of his grandson dangled, in indignation.

"By the whole sentence!" said Mr. Parkhill.

"But couldn't Number One mean Number Two, and Number Two mean Number One?" demanded Goldie Pomeranz.

"Soitinly!" Mr. Kaplan hailed the horror as if it were a blessing.

"Yes, Miss Pomeranz. That's my point! By *themselves,* we cannot tell if 'Interest' Number One means 'Interest' Number Two. It's the *sentence* in which each word is used that tells us beyond doubt which meaning is right. Suppose I say, 'He interests the class.' That's very different from my saying 'He went to the bank and received the interest on his money!"

"Thata I like," said Miss Caravello.

"Splendid axemple!" said Mr. Kaplan.

"There's *no* way of mistaking the meaning of 'Interest' Number One and 'Interest' Number Two in *those* sentences, is there?"

"No!"

"Never!"

"It's the sentence, not the woid!" blushed Miss Mitnick.

"Exactly. And here is a final example!" Mr. Parkhill stepped to the right end of the board cheerfully, thinking that in teaching as in life, goblins seen are goblins slain. He printed:

## 1. SWALLOW
## 2. SWALLOW

The third pair of homonyms refanned the fires of chaos.

"Too much!"

"Not fair!"

"I'll—ne-ver—agree!"

This time Mrs. Moskowitz's "Ooo-oy!" was the wheeze of a woman about to become a corpse.

"But this is a rather *amusing* example," Mr. Parkhill put in lightly. (Plaut and Samish never tired of encouraging teachers to inject humor into workaday tasks.) " 'Swallow' Number One is a movement in the throat—this way . . ." He produced a monumental ingurgitation. "But 'Swallow' Number Two is a bird!"

"Why," objected Mr. Pinsky, "can't 'Swallow' Number *One* be a boid and 'Swallow' Number *Two* be a—" He almost dislocated his Adam's apple.

"Oh, they can!" exclaimed Mr. Parkhill. "That's very good, sir. It is the way we *use* the words which tells us the difference. For instance, 'She swallowed the ice cream' tells us instantly that 'swallow' means"—he swallowed—"whereas 'She saw the swallow' tells us that she saw a bird! Do you see how *completely* the meaning is conveyed by the whole sentence?!"

"Absolutely!"

"No doubts!"

"Mr. Pockheel is a ginius!" proclaimed Mr. Kaplan.

Mr. Parkhill placed the chalk (how quickly it had become a stub) into the trough on the ledge. "Well, class, see how much we have accomplished!"

Joy reigned, albeit confined.

"Qvastion!" It was Mr. Kaplan.

Mr. Parkhill braced himself. "Y-yes?"

"I unnistand avery single pot you axplained so fine. Still, vun point bodders me. . . ."

Mr. Parkhill wiped the chalk dust off his fingers. "Y-yes?"

"Soppose I use a santance wit' 'Svallow' Number Vun an' *also* 'Svallow' Number Two?"

Mr. Parkhill frowned. "I fail to see—"

"Vell," asked Mr. Kaplan, "ken't a svallow svallow?"

Mr. Parkhill's head began to ache.

"Stop!" bawled Norman Bloom.

"Shame . . . shame . . ." knelled Miss Tarnova.

"I think I leave this class!" announced Mr. Scymczak.

"*I* thinka I'll taka poison!" glowered Carmen Caravello.

"Mr. Kaplan happens to be right," said Mr. Parkhill. "One *can* use a sentence with both meanings. Er—'I saw the swallow swallow the seed,' for instance, or 'Why can't the swallow swallow?' "

"Next Keplan will want a word with *three* meanings!" warned Aaron Blattberg.

"Aren't tweens enough, Koplan?" snorted Mr. Perez. "Treeples you want, yet? In English are no—"

Mr. Parkhill did not know what to say. English does, of course, contain quite a number of triple homonyms (or homophones, for that matter). He would have been delighted to take his pilgrims through the enticing guises of that one syllable which is identical for "air" and "heir" and "err." He visualized a board on which glowed:

> We breathe *air.*
> To *err* is human, to forgive divine!
> A child is an *heir.*

Why he could even have conjured up a sentence with a delightful triple-decker:

> The *heir erred* when he left the lawyer's office for a breath of *air!*

39

"I think we had better leave the three-meaninged words for a later session," he heard himself saying. "Perhaps near the—very end of the semester."

There was no point in pushing fate too hard. He had survived the passage between Scylla and Charybdis. But Poseidon's trident had fearful prongs. . . .

"Please turn to page sixty-one of our text. . . ."

Sometimes Mr. Parkhill wished he had become a teacher of arithmetic.

# 4

## THE ASTOUNDING BIRTH OF
## NATHAN P. NATHAN

"Mr. Aaron Blattberg."

"Right here!"

"Miss Fanny Gidwitz."

"In place."

"Mr. Matsoukas."

"Ugh!"

"Mr. Nathan P. Nathan."

"Yes, *sir!* Ready and willing!"

Mr. Parkhill looked up, smiling. He rather liked young Nathan P. Nathan. This was only Mr. Nathan's third appearance in the beginners' grade. He had not registered until six weeks after the fall session had begun. But that was not unusual. The American Night Preparatory School for Adults prided itself upon its adaptability.

Nathan P. Nathan surely was no newcomer to our shores. He spoke fluent English. He used idioms with ease and colloquial phrases with abandon. He did not flinch before the wayward vernacular which tormented so many members of the beginners' grade, nor the baffling locutions which plunged so many into despair.

Everyone in the class liked Mr. Nathan. He was an energetic redhead, no more than twenty-three or -four, bubbly in manner, swift of speech. And Mr. Nathan laughed. He always laughed. He seemed to be the happiest young man on earth. His was an infectious laugh. Even Hyman Kaplan, who did not wear his heart on his sleeve, chuckled with comradely pleasure when Nathan P. Nathan laughed.

One more characteristic distinguished Mr. Nathan from all the other members of the class. He wore nothing over his sweater, no matter what the temperature outside. (The sweater had two yellow stripes running down the right side, and a thick, chenille "C.N.S." on the left pocket: the initials stood for "Cholisk's Net Sharks," the name of Mr. Nathan's basketball team, which was emblazoned *in toto* on the back.) Young Nathan always removed that sweater the moment he entered the classroom. He sat soaking up knowledge, with the utmost elation, in a short-sleeved shirt. Beneath and beyond those shortened sleeves, biceps the size of potatoes bulged, muscles of such pleasing size and grace that they were often eyed in sidelong yearning by Miss Tarnova.

The one thing that puzzled Mr. Parkhill about Nathan P. Nathan was that he never did homework. He always gave a plausible excuse: "I worked overtime"; "My uncle was sick"; "I had to visit my sister in Patchogue." And Mr. Nathan always found some reason not to go to the blackboard when his name was called: "My wrist is sprained"; "My corns are killing me!"; "I strained last night my back in basketball." (Mr. Nathan would no more think of skipping a basketball game, in the Lefkowitz League, than Miss Goldberg would think of renouncing her Milky Ways. He had the highest absentee record in the grade, and Miss Schnepfe, in the principal's office, had written him—and Mr. Parkhill—several severe notes about it.)

Now, it was the third Recitation and Speech exercise of the semester. Mr. Parkhill had devoted the preceding session to Dangling Participles. But to his students, Recitation and Speech constituted an ordeal far greater than dangling participles, because of the intensely personal character of Recitation, its demands on the poise, the confidence, the sheer recuperative speed of a lone pupil exposed to public dissection. The class was merciless when it came to criticizing a student's performance in Recitation and Speech.

The evening had opened rather well, with Mr. Wolfgang Schmitt's speech on Goethe, whose poems ("in ze orichinal Cherman") Mr. Schmitt extolled as second to none. "Cookie" Kipnis had followed Mr. Schmitt with a lively anecdote involving a *contretemps* whilst "shopping at Gimpel's," which she patronized when not loyal to "Mazy's." Miss Gerta Valuskas had recited a moving poem in Finnish, which she translated with elocutionary gestures that held her peers in thrall. (But since no one in the class knew a word of Finnish, there was no telling how accurate Miss Valuskas's translation really was—and no point, therefore, in criticizing her English version.) Mr. Finsterwald had presented what seemed an eloquent eulogy to Holland—until a reference to Beersheba made it dawn upon his mystified colleagues that Karl Finsterwald was talking not about Holland but the Holy Land.

Suddenly, Mr. Parkhill decided to call upon Mr. Nathan. He smiled invitingly as he said, "Mr. Nathan, don't you think it's about time *you* addressed us? I mean," he swiftly added, "if you feel up to it."

"I'm fit as a fiddle and happy to oblige," laughed Nathan P. Nathan.

The announcement elicited surprised "Ah"s and pleased "Oh"s and Mr. Kaplan's benedictory, "Good boy! Ve all stend besite yoursalf!"

Mr. Nathan laughed once more. His red head bobbed toward the front platform, which he reached with the leap of a hurdler. (He certainly was a healthy young man.) "Hello, folks, hello!" trumpeted Mr. Nathan. "I will talk short and to the point. My name is Nathan P. Nathan and I am twenty-four years old and I was born on a train—"

A gasp escaped Mrs. Yanoff.

"—by my mother, an anagel, God bless her memory—"

*"Aleha ha-shalom."* Mr. Pinsky honored the departed.

"—and my father was a furrier in Odessa but he ran away to Turkey and then Engaland, where he met and got married to my mother, God bless her, and I started school in New York but we were poor so I had to stop in the six garade and go to work to help out and give every penny to my mother, a woman a saint, now in heaven—"

"She should rest in peace," called Mrs. Shimmelfarb.

"—and my first job was pushing carts in the garament distarict, then packing bundles for a boss a *murderer,* and now I stuff pillows. I push in them kapok, *piles* of kapok, eight hours a day and half-day Saturday—"

"Shame," hissed Mr. Marcus, who was extremely pious.

"—but I don't mind as the pay is good and all the guys at work are peachy. And now I come to school because— well, because even if you think my talking of English sounds good—"

"Like an American-born!" cried Miss Gidwitz.

"—I don't *read* so good, and my spelling is from hunger. So I want to learn to read and spell my father should be paroud of me. I hope every other cripple in this room will also learn perfect. Thank you, ladies. Thank you, gentlemen. Thank you, Mr. Parkhill." Laughing, dancing like a boxer, his short sleeves fluttering, the exuberant young man bounced back to his seat.

"Vunderful spitch!" cried Mr. Kaplan.

"Oh, Mr. *Nathan,*" breathed Miss Mitnick.

"Bravo!" sang Carmen Caravello. *"Bravissimo!"*

"A plashure!" crowed Mrs. Moskowitz, for once forsaking the shades of Cimmeria.

"Mr. Nathan, that was excellent—" began Mr. Parkhill, but Hyman Kaplan, heretofore unrivaled for ebullience, turned to bubbling Nathan and declaimed: "I don't care if you vere born in a sobvay, boychik, you made a spitch you should be prod! But don't call de cless 'cripples.' Dat's not nice. Say better 'greenhorns.' Still—"

"Mr. Kap—"

"—congradulation, Nat'an P. Nat'an! Congradulation, class, we should have soch a student! Congradulation to de school, an American-born should comm here! Cong—"

There was no telling how many persons or institutions Mr. Kaplan intended to congratulate, for the recess bell was trilling like a nightingale.

The post-recess comments on Mr. Nathan's oration were (at least, so they started) as brief as they were generous.

"It was a wonderful speech," blushed Miss Mitnick, "although you don't have to say 'anagel' for 'angel,' or 'garade' for 'grade.' "

"Mr. Parkhill is not Mr. Par*ak*hill," Miss Ziev primly observed.

"Why give each word free syllable?" sulked Gus Matsoukas.

"It's a habit," laughed Nathan P. Nathan.

"Change it!" snapped Mr. Blattberg.

"I learned it from my *father*. He talks like that."

"Then don't change! Respact your father!" called Mr. Pinsky. "It won't hoit the language."

"How old is your papa?" asked Mrs. Tomasic hopefully.

"Class—" Mr. Parkhill started. "I think—"

"Where was thees train going?" piped Vincente Perez.

*"Which* tren?" asked Miss Schneiderman.

"Thees train he was born on eet!"

"I don't know," laughed Mr. Nathan.

The room was thrown into consternation.

*"You don't know where you were borned?!"* moaned Mrs. Moskowitz.

45

"No one did tell you if you are an Englisher, a Sviss, even a Toik?" asked Mr. Vinograd.

"Class—"

"Nobody *knew,*" pealed Nathan P. Nathan. "We were in a big hurry. My father took the first train he could throw the whole family on."

"In which *contry?*" appealed Miss Gidwitz.

"Canada."

*"Canada?!"* gulped Mr. Scymczak, who confused it with Australia.

"So he's not an American!" Miss Goldberg's disappointment was so great that she ate two squares of butterscotch.

"So he's a Canadian!" called Mr. Kaplan. *"I* should be so locky!"

Mr. Parkhill drummed on the table many times before he could calm the heated forum. "Class, I do think we should return to the *English* aspects of Mr. Nathan's recita—"

"Isn't being a nativer more important than he puts in extra syllables?" That was Norman Bloom, prickly as ever.

"Well—"

"Nat'an P. Nat'an," Mr. Kaplan suddenly blurted, "vhat does it say on your birth stiff-ticket?!"

" 'Cer*ti*ficate,' Mr. Kaplan, not 'stiff—' "

"I haven't got a birth ceratificate," laughed Mr. Nathan.

"What?!"

"No!"

"A scendal!"

"Ain't you ashame?"

Sympathy for young Nathan mingled with reproaches to the authorities in Washington, Ottawa, and several wholly uninvolved capitals.

"It's a *crime* America shouldn't give a boith paper to a baby who was born—"

"How do we know he wasn't born in *Alaska?*" demanded Mr. Blattberg. "How do you know he ain't an Eskimal?"

"Our train didn't go through Alaska," laughed Mr. Nathan. "We carossed Niagara Falls. And that's when I was born."

A camel playing the bagpipes would have caused no greater sensation.

"On Niakra Falls?! One of de world's natural wonderfuls?!"

"You got born on a *britch?!*" exclaimed Mr. Pinsky.

"Class—"

"Did you see it?"

"Don't be a silly!" scoffed Mrs. Moskowitz, a veteran of two parturitions. "He wasn't *born* in time to see—"

"Ladies—"

"Maybe he was!" crooned Olga Tarnova. "Maybe his forst look on worrld was Niogora Falls!"

"I couldn't see for a month!" beamed Mr. Nathan.

"Maybe just a peek out the window?" pouted Miss Tarnova.

Mr. Nathan rocked with delight. "You have to remember that I don't know if I was inside or outside my mother when we carossed the Falls!"

"Omig*ott!*" mourned Mr. Feigenbaum.

"That's true," said Mrs. Yanoff.

"Sod, sod," moaned Olga Tarnova.

*"Class—"*

"Vait!" Mr. Kaplan leaped to his feet, clutching one lapel in the manner of Daniel Webster. "Nat'an P. Nat'an, hear mine voids! *T'ink!* T'ink vary hod, vary careful! Exectly vhere—"

"Mr. Kaplan—"

"—did you breed in your vary foist brat?"

"In the middle of the bridge," bubbled Mr. Nathan.

Astonishment grappled with disbelief amongst the confused geographers. The room rocked between horror and incredulity.

"Ladies . . . Gentlemen . . ."

47

"You could be a citizen of a *britch?!*" gasped Mr. Kaplan.

"Poor Mr. Nathan," sighed Miss Mitnick.

"A bridge is not a country!" protested Miss Valuskas. "Everyone has to be born in a *country!*"

"I didn't choose it," laughed Mr. Nathan.

"Some people are born on boats!" blurted Mrs. Yanoff. "My brother's Sammy fell don on de dack—"

"My seester was born eeen a airaplane!" exclaimed Mr. Perez.

"Class—"

"Stop!" boomed Mr. Bloom. "Ain't we all jumping on conclusions? How does the rad-had *know* his first brath of air was on that train? He was just born! Probly cryink like crazy. Who *told* him he began to breed on a bridge in the middle of—"

"The conductor," grinned Mr. Nathan.

"A *condoctor?!*" Mrs. Moskowitz could not believe her ears.

"Maybe de condoctor made de delivery!" exclaimed Mr. Kaplan.

"No," laughed Nathan P. Nathan. "My mother did it alone."

*"Alone?!"*

"No doctor? No noises?"

"Hows about your *fadder?*" asked Mr. Kaplan. "He didn't tell you? He vas prazant!"

"My father fainted. The minute my mother's labor pains began."

"So conzolt your mother!" blared Mr. Blattberg.

"He can't, dummy! Did you forgot she pessed avay?"

*"Aleha ha-shalom,"* incanted Mr. Pinsky.

"Class, I *must* insist that we drop this entire line of— discussion!" Mr. Parkhill rapped the knuckles of both hands on his chair until they throbbed. "However fascinating the question of Mr. Nathan's birth may be—and

48

I should be the last to deny it is a—most intriguing case—I think we should return to our studies! Let us go back to Mr. Nathan's recitation. Look at any mistakes you wrote down at the time—or any improvements you care to suggest."

It was not easy to wrench adults, absorbed in an extraordinary nativity on the bridge over Niagara Falls, back to trivial missteps in enunciation—especially since the recitation of Nathan P. Nathan had displayed such a stellar range, such a fluent command of so spacious an English vocabulary, that any member of the class would gladly have changed places with him.

"Who would like to start us off all over again?" asked Mr. Parkhill. "Mr. Trabish?"

Mr. Trabish, having dozed throughout the whole drama of Mr. Nathan's mobile delivery, was jabbed in the ribs by Mr. Scymczak, only to ask, "What time is it?"

Mr. Parkhill frowned. "Mrs.—Shimmelfarb?"

Mrs. Shimmelfarb said, "I don't like that Mr. Nathan called his boss a murderer!"

"He was a crook also," laughed Mr. Nathan. "He went to jail!"

"Miss Gidwitz?" said Mr. Parkhill swiftly. (Who knew what a furor Mr. Nathan's past employer might cause?)

"In Mr. Nathan's fest speech, he said 'guys,'" said Miss Gidwitz, "instead of 'boys,' 'men,' or 'other workers.' The word 'guys' is sleng!"

"Quite so," said Mr. Parkhill. "'Guys' is slang—"

"I *like* slang," beamed Mr. Nathan.

"*I* like '*shlemiel*' but I don't say it in the class!" said Mrs. Yanoff.

"What means '*shlemiel*'?" growled Mr. Wilkomirski.

"Class! . . . Miss Pomeranz?"

"Mr. Nathan spoke very, very nice, with good words all over," sighed Miss Pomeranz. "But I think he should not

49

make a whole speech one-two-three, using such long sentences!"

"They were very good sentences," ventured Miss Mitnick.

"But he should stop at least for periods!" complained Miss Pomeranz. "And he should *wait* for commas, semicolons, and so for."

"That is a very helpful suggestion," said Mr. Parkhill. "Mr. Nathan, you do have a tendency to run your sentences together."

"Agreed!" Mr. Nathan chuckled. "That's why I'm in school. I never learned about stopping for periods, or waiting for commas, because at home we all talk so fast you can't get in a word hatch-wise."

"Er—it's 'edge-wise,' not 'hatch-wise,'" said Mr. Parkhill.

"'Edgewise'!" exulted Mr. Nathan. "Already I learned!"

"Nat'an!" called out Mr. Kaplan, who had been silent for a good four minutes. "Did you aver vote?"

"Sure."

"You *voted?*"

"Why not? I'm an American."

"How do you know you're not a Nigerian?" scoffed Mr. Bloom.

*"I'll* esk de qvestions," said Mr. Kaplan. "Nat'an, to vote you got to give full ditails—"

"I did."

"So vhere dey esk 'Place of Birth,' *vhat did you put don?"*

"Pullman."

This brought new pandemonium into the room.

"Pullman!"

"Is that a city?"

"In U.S.?"

"A state?"

50

"Mr. Pockhall," intoned Miss Tarnova, "is there soch a place?"

Mr. Parkhill said, "I think that when Mr. Nathan said 'Pullman' he meant that he was born on a Pullman *train.*"

"Fa goodness sek!"

"Trains have *names?*" blinked Mr. Schmitt.

"Well, the individual cars in a train do," explained Mr. Parkhill. "They are often named after an American hero, or an Indian tribe—"

"Hindyans had trains?" gaped Mrs. Yanoff. "I thought they had only horses and toupees!"

" 'T*e*pees,' not 'tou—' "

"So dat's vhy his name is Nat'an P. Nat'an!" cried Mr. Kaplan. "De 'P' is for 'Pullman'!"

"Right!" laughed Mr. Nathan.

"So Nat'an P. Nat'an vas telling de ebsolute troot," declaimed Mr. Kaplan. "He vas born in a Pullman! He also *sad* he vas born dere. He jost laft ot de article 'a.' "

"No tricks!" boomed Mr. Blattberg. *"Is* there a rill place called Pullman? Or is the American government giving citizenship to *beds* and wagons—"

"Class!" Mr. Parkhill's voice ascended with force from the stand on which the unabridged dictionary—rarely consulted—reclined. He had been consulting the gazetteer. "Yes! There is a city named Pullman! It is in the state of Washington. And there *was* a suburb of Chicago named Pullman, where the sleeping-car Pullman coaches were originally manufactured!"

"Hooray!" cried Mr. Kaplan. "Nat'an P. Nat'an is no liar! In fect, he has a choice! Born in Chicago—"

"He's too young!"

"—or Vashington! I vote for Vashington!"

Mr. Nathan was shaking with jubilation. "I agree. I did. When I voted the first time, which was last year, and they asked of me, 'Where were you born?' I said 'Pullman.' The

51

lady clerk said, 'Ah, in the state of Washington. That's where my husband comes from.' I didn't deny."

"Good for you!"

"Smart!"

"So she asked if I had a birth certificate."

"Oh!"

"No!"

"What you *did?*"

Mr. Nathan laughed. "I said my father had my birth certificate, which is true. But I told them he was back in Canada, which he was at that time, working in the rush fur season."

"Not so fast!" stormed Mr. Blattberg. "Nathan was very clever—but I say it's not ligal! A boy born on a train, over vater, not on the dirt and soil of U.S.—"

"Doesn't a baby born on a train have *rights?*" cried Mr. Kaplan. "Is a child a box garlic? Ve—"

"Mr. Kap—"

"—ve have a Constitution! If Nat'an P. Nat'an vas born *vun inch* insite our borders—"

"Kaplan siddon!" fumed Norman Bloom.

"Kaplan, kip on!" called loyal Pinsky.

"Nat'an," continued Mr. Kaplan, "just enswer vun point: Did you ritch insite U.S. in time you should be a *born citizen?*"

"That's what no one knows," laughed Mr. Nathan.

"Class—"

"Soch a chence to miss. By vun minute—de most, maybe hefenarr!" ("Heffenarr" was Mr. Kaplan's way of designating thirty minutes.)

"Class, I hate to end this discussion!" announced Mr. Parkhill. "But it is almost time to leave. I—want to add just a few comments to Mr. Nathan's recitation. You said, if I remember correctly, 'my talking of English.' Would it not be better to—"

"De enswer!" cried Hyman Kaplan. "I got de enswer! Nat'an—"

"Mr. Kap—"

"De train you vere on! T'ink! Vas it goink tovard de U.S. or tovard Canada?"

Mr. Nathan was so pleased that he slapped his thigh. "We were coming from Canada, so we were going to America!"

"Dat's all! Dat's inoff! Ve'll appil to de Supreme Cawt if ve nidd to!" Never had Hyman Kaplan been so magisterial. "A train goink *to* a place minns dat de pipple on dat train got on axpactink to *go* to dat place! So if you vere born *bifore* you pessed across de border of Canada, dat vould be too bed, a tarrible mistake! But if you *pessed* Canada and vere movink *tovard* de U.S., your modder and fodder ebsolutely axpacted you vould be born on Amarican soil! *Axpactink* is de point! It shows—"

It mattered not that the bell had rung while Mr. Kaplan was still approaching the American border; no one had heard, much less heeded, it.

"*—you are a citizen becawss you vere born in U.S.A.!* Congradulation, Citizen Nat'an P. Nat'an!"

Mr. Nathan was laughing and shaking and holding his sides. "Mr. Kaplan, you are a peach. An okay guy! I'll tell my father."

"Keplen is a born lawyer!" proclaimed Mr. Pinsky.

"Did you say 'lawyer' or 'liar'?" howled Norman Bloom.

"Dipands on who he mant," said Mr. Kaplan.

The bell was still belling authoritatively as the congregation swept out of the room, babbling and excited, Nathan P. Nathan in the center of the congratulatory throng. Miss Mitnick tiptoed along the edge, blushing. Someone shouted, "This was the most intarasting class we ever had!"

"Denk you," said Mr. Kaplan.

Mr. Parkhill sank into his chair. The room was blessedly quiet. Slowly, he took off his glasses. He rubbed his eyes. He was exhausted.

He was also confused. How in the world could he have known that a prosaic Recitation and Speech drill would turn into the stormy case of Kaplan *vs.* the U.S. Bureau of Immigration?

# 5

## THE FIFTY MOODS
## OF MR. PARKHILL

Mr. Parkhill entered the classroom at 6:30, a full hour before the class would begin. He would have entered even earlier, but Mr. Janowitz, the school "custodian," was absolutely adamant about sweeping the floors and washing down the blackboards.

Mr. Parkhill could hardly wait (as he had to, in the corridor) to get to those blackboards. The moment morose Mr. Janowitz said, "Is finish," Mr. Parkhill hurried in. He took his "WORK" folder out of his briefcase and approached the gleaming slates. He was rather excited as he lifted a stick of fresh chalk. (Mr. Janowitz distributed fresh, full pieces of chalk along the ledges at the beginning of each week—and only at the beginning of each week, ever since Mr. Robinson had reproached the faculty: "The amount of chalk we are all using is enough to build the white cliffs of Dover!" Not many principals could put things as graphically as that.)

This was the dawn of a new week. Throughout the entire weekend, one idea had driven all others out of Mr. Parkhill's mind. . . . In capital letters, Mr. Parkhill swiftly printed, on the top of the board at the far left:

He balanced the folder in his left hand and, smiling, transcribed:

1. We *move.*
2.      "   *are going to move.*
3.      "   *are moving.*
4.      "   *moved.*
5.      "   *did move.*
6.      "   *had moved.*
7.      "   *had been moved.*
8.      "   *shall move.*
9.      "   *shall be moving.*
10.     "   *shall have moved.*

Mr. Parkhill stepped to the next board.

11. We *shall have been moved.*
12.     "   *will move.*
13.     "   *will be moving.*
14.     "   *will have moved.*
15.     "   *will have been moved.*
16.     "   *may move.*
17.     "   *may be moving.*
18.     "   *may have moved.*
19.     "   *may have been moved.*

Now Mr. Parkhill stepped one board farther to the right.

20. We *can move.*
21.     "   *can be moving.*
22.     "   *can have moved.*
23.     "   *can have been moved.*
24.     "   *could move.*
25.     "   *could be moving.*
26.     "   *could have moved.*
27.     "   *could have been moved.*

28.   "  *might move.*
29.   "  *might be moving.*
30.   "  *might have moved.*
31.   "  *might have been moved.*

Mr. Parkhill moved to the next blackboard.

32. We *ought to move.*
33.   "  *ought to be moving.*
34.   "  *ought to have moved.*
35.   "  *ought to have been moved.*
36.   "  *should move.*
37.   "  *should be moving.*
38.   "  *should have moved.*
39.   "  *should have been moved.*

Mr. Parkhill paused, rubbing the numbness out of his forefinger, then resumed writing on the blackboard in the corner, at right angles to the three he had filled:

40. We *will move.*
41.   "  *will be moving.*
42.   "  *will have moved.*
43.   "  *will have been moved.*
44.   "  *must move.*
45.   "  *must be moving.*
46.   "  *must have moved.*
47.   "  *must have been moved.*
48.   "  *have to move.*
49.   "  *have to be moving.*
50.   "  *have to have been moved.*

Exhilarated, and slightly exhausted, Mr. Parkhill placed the depleted chalk in the trough. Fifty examples! His eyes scanned them swiftly, and not without pride. *Fifty* examples! Mr. Parkhill rather wished that Mr. Robinson would drop into the classroom tonight, as he sometimes did, on one of his unannounced rounds of inspection.

Fifty examples—and, Mr. Parkhill reflected, he had not

even included "We have got to move" or "We have got to be moving" or even "We have got to have been moved!" He had not included them because he wholeheartedly agreed with that telling passage in Plaut and Samish:

> . . . newcomers to our shores are often discouraged, and sometimes severely depressed, by *an over-dose of examples.* Just as a seasoned physician administers a measured amount of even the best medication to a patient, knowing the dangers which may attend a larger (even fatal) quantum of medicaments, so the teacher must guard against that exuberance which tempts him, no less than the physician, to use a "shotgun" where prudence dictates *"satis superque."* Indeed, enough is often more than enough!

Fifty examples . . . Mr. Parkhill hoped he had not been carried away by his optimism. This was not at all the employment of "a shotgun," which sprays many identical bullets at one target. Each example on those blackboards was different from its companions; each was a case in its own right; each stood on its own feet and asserted its own exact meaning. How, Mr. Parkhill reassured himself, could a true survey of tenses and moods omit the pluperfect, for instance, or turn a deaf ear to the subjunctive? And what better way was there to show his students how marvelous, how rich and various and supple, are the resources of the language they strove so valiantly to master?

Fifty examples . . . They stretched across all the boards in the room. They stood arrayed, sound and confident, like —well, like fine soldiers on a parade ground. Mr. Parkhill smiled. His misgivings dissolved. He straightened his vest.

A peculiar sound, as from someone being strangled, caused him to turn. He had not heard the student come into the room. It was Mr. Scymczak. But Mr. Scymczak was not in his usual seat (on the aisle, third row). Mr. Scymczak was leaning against the wall, the color of an artichoke.

58

"Good evening," smiled Mr. Parkhill.

No comprehensible syllable interrupted the noises of asphyxiation. Mr. Scymczak's hat was clutched in one hand, his textbook hung inert from the other.

"Mr. Scymczak . . ."

Hoarse rattlings breached the gates of those bloodless lips.

"Mr. Scymczak!" exclaimed Mr. Parkhill in alarm.

The plasterer from Danzig rolled his eyeballs and, with either a sob or a whimper, staggered out of the room.

"Mr. Scymczak! Please! Don't go—"

All Mr. Parkhill heard was shoes clattering down the corridor. He sank into his chair. What on earth . . . He rather *liked* Mr. Scymczak. Could it be that—

"Goot ivnink!" a cheerful tenor sang out.

Mr. Parkhill glanced up. "Oh. Good evening, Mr. Kaplan."

Mr. Kaplan waved his hand with customary éclat and strode, humming, to his undisputed throne in the center of the front row. He sat down, placed his composition book on the arm of the chair, arranged his pencils and crayons, and brightly glanced at the board. The next thing Mr. Parkhill knew, Hyman Kaplan was sliding down his seat, the smile seeping off his lips.

"Mr. Kaplan! What's wrong?"

The stricken scholar gurgled. His head rotated as his glassy eyes traversed Moods 11 through 19.

Suddenly, Miss Higby poked her head through the open doorway. "Mr. Park—" She did not complete the name. Never before had Mr. Parkhill seen such an expression on Miss Higby's features. She looked as though she had just been embalmed. She was not looking at him. She was goggling at the blackboards.

Quickly, Mr. Parkhill said, "I thought I'd give the class a thorough overview of the many tenses and moods—"

59

"Fifty?!" gasped his colleague.

"—to demonstrate the remarkable range—"

"You have! Oh, you *have!*" And without another word, Miss Higby dropped a pink memo on his desk and bolted away.

Mr. Parkhill frowned. He leaned back in his chair. The clock on the wall sounded like a trip-hammer beating on brass. The expression on Washington's noble lithograph seemed to have curdled; the countenance of merciful Lincoln appeared to have turned aghast.

Mr. Parkhill cleared his throat. He glanced at Mr. Kaplan, who was almost horizontal in his chair. "Er—Mr. Kaplan—" To his annoyance, Mr. Parkhill's voice was hoarse.

Mr. Kaplan's hearing was no more alive than his posture.

"Mr. Kaplan," said Mr. Parkhill more loudly.

The recumbent figure quivered.

"Mr. Kaplan, may I ask you a—candid question?"

The candidate for a candid question thrashed about as if extricating himself from a straitjacket, the activity changing the color in his cheeks from none to a shade of oatmeal.

"Mr. Kaplan, do you think—please be honest!—that I have—er—overdone the examples?"

"Dey are amazink . . ."

"Thank you. But do you think I have given too many?"

Mr. Kaplan blinked. He gulped. He started to produce a gurgle when the door opened and Rochelle Goldberg, as pert as she was plump, materialized in the doorway.

"Goldboig, don't faint!" cried Mr. Kaplan.

"Huh?"

"Don't look on de boards!"

That was all Miss Goldberg needed to turn to the blackboards.

"Miss Goldberg—" began Mr. Parkhill. "I—Miss Goldberg!!"

Miss Goldberg had not fainted. She had not even reeled. All she had done was drop her jaw, her books, her handbag, and a bag of jellybeans. (Why Miss Goldberg had chosen this particular evening to lay in a restorative stock of jellybeans, instead of her customary nougats, caramels, or Hershey "Kisses," Mr. Parkhill knew he would never know. He could not help it if *"Deus est qui regit omnia"* flashed into his mind.) Those infernal oblates splattered across the floor and bounded around like Mexican jumping beans: yellow, pink, white, brown. . . .

Mr. Kaplan cried, "I varned you!" and fell to his knees. So did Miss Goldberg. Mr. Parkhill could hardly refuse to join them in the imperative task. The three of them scrambled about snatching at the confections, which were rolling around on the floor and under the chairs as if the classroom were a pinball machine.

"Excuse me, oh"—poor Miss Goldberg was stammering —"I'm vary sorry—"

"It's quite all right," said Mr. Parkhill.

"Even I hev eccidents," Mr. Kaplan admitted.

"I'm so embarrassed!"

"You need not be, Miss Goldberg. Not at *all*—"

"Naxt time, drop gum," advised Mr. Kaplan. "Gum don't bounce arond like mobbles."

"It's not *polite* to chew gum in class," bleated Miss Goldberg.

"It's not polite to make Mr. Pockheel sqvash colors all over his pants!"

Mr. Parkhill's knees were indeed acquiring the hues of a sticky palette. "Oh, don't mind that. I should have sent this suit to the cleaner's months ago."

At last the floor was cleared by six strong hands. Mr. Parkhill rose, smiling bravely. Mr. Kaplan rose, glancing sourly at Miss Goldberg, who rose, announcing, "I have to go to the ladies' room."

"Please come back," said Mr. Parkhill.

"Duty is duty!" scowled Mr. Kaplan.

Miss Goldberg was halfway to her refuge.

*"Well . . ."* Mr. Parkhill began dusting his trousers, then wiping the stickiness off his hands. "As I was saying, before this unfortunate interruption . . ." He paused. "I have a feeling I placed too much on those boards!"

Mr. Kaplan sighed.

Mr. Parkhill blurted, "Do you think it would be wise to remove—"

"De nombers," said Mr. Kaplan.

"I beg your pardon?"

"Take avay all de nombers."

Mr. Parkhill knit his brow. "You think I should erase all of the *numbers?*"

"Positively. If Moskowitz—just take a 'for instence'—gats vun look at a nomber like *fifty,* she'll have a hot atteck."

"Oh." Mr. Parkhill adjusted his spectacles. "I suppose I *could* omit the numbers after, say, forty—"

"I soggest all de nombers."

*"All* of the numbers?" echoed Mr. Parkhill in pain.

"All."

"But—"

"Mr. Pockheel," said Mr. Kaplan with a certain patience, "look. If you take a boy for a valk, you don't say, 'Let's valk fife miles.' De kit vould say, *'Vhat?!* Fife miles? I ken't!' So you say, 'Let's take a valk—a nice valk, maybe a *long* valk. . . .'"

Mr. Parkhill stepped to the board without a word. He made a series of powerful down-strokes with the eraser, expunging ninety-one numerals within nine seconds. "Yes, that *is* better . . . Uh—I shall be happy to have any other suggestions, Mr. Kaplan."

Mr. Kaplan beamed. "It's an honor."

"After all, you are more—objective than I can be."

"I don't *object!* You a vunderful titcher! It's not my place—"

"I mean, you can see the—total impression in a way I cannot. You can see the woods as well as the trees! What else would you do?"

Mr. Kaplan made an apologetic twitch. "I don't vant to sond like a student knows batter den Mr. Pockheel . . ."

"Speak frankly, please!"

The sage closed one eye. "I also vould cot ot a bushel of all dose exemples."

"That *many?*"

"More than many! Wholesale!"

"Oh . . . Which examples would you erase?"

Mr. Kaplan rubbed his chin. "In voibs, vhat does de beginnis' cless nidd? Just de prazant tanse, de pest, an' de future. Dat's enof for a lifetime!"

Mr. Parkhill tried to repress his dismay. "You mean you would erase all of the tenses except past, present, and future?!"

"Mit' plashure."

"But so many of the other tenses—and moods—are so valuable!"

"Bendages are weluable, too," mused Mr. Kaplan, *"if* you are bliddink. But if you are not bliddink, iven in a finger, vhy bendage op de whole hend?"

Mr. Parkhill gazed with falling affection and failing pride upon that impressive aggregation: the staunch "shall have"s, the bold "shall have been"s. He felt awful. "But if I erase all of the examples except—"

"Prazant, pest, future."

"—there will remain—only three sentences!"

Mr. Kaplan shrugged. "So? De hongry don't nidd a benqvet. Sometimes a sendvich is batter den a fist!"

"I think you mean 'feast,' Mr. Kaplan, not 'fist.' "

63

"Denk you."

Mr. Parkhill turned to the blackboard. "Can't we leave more than just three sentences? Just a few others? I mean, the most necessary—"

"Vhich vuns?"

"Well, 'We are moving,' for instance. That is *very* important! And 'We *will* be moving.' And—"

"Dose," agreed Mr. Kaplan, "are weluable."

"I do think we should retain those!" said Mr. Parkhill earnestly.

"Agreet," said Mr. Kaplan.

With broad, sweeping strokes of the eraser, and sad sinkings of regret in his heart, Mr. Parkhill wiped out every syllable he had written on the five boards. He exchanged eraser for chalk, and as Mr. Kaplan made little clucks of approval, wrote:

We move.
" are moving.
" moved.
" were moving.
" will move.
" will be moving.

Mr. Parkhill placed the chalk against his lips, concentrating. "That certainly is simpler. . . ."

"It's movvelous! . . . Now put in nombers."

"Numbers?"

"Ufcawss!"

"But I thought you criticized the numbers—"

"I objected to de *number* of nombers. Now are only six. Bifore vere *fifty!*"

"But—"

"*Fifty* makes dizzy. But *six*? Dat gives de cless *hope!*"

Mr. Parkhill placed "1, 2, 3, 4, 5, 6" on the board.

Not until the session was over that night (the lesson went extremely well) did Mr. Parkhill remember to read the pink sheet Miss Higby had handed him so long—so very long—ago.

### *To The Faculty*

In my remarks of the 17th inst., I stressed the need for drastic economy in the use of chalk. I neglected to point out that a reduction in the amount of chalk used on our blackboards will effect a corresponding economy in the wear-and-tear of our erasers!

I trust every member of the faculty will henceforth bear this in mind!

*Leland Robinson*
Principal

# 6

## MR. K·A·P·L·A·N
## WRESTLES THE "W"

Mr. Parkhill was troubled about "v"s and "w"s. For weeks he had known that something would have to be done about them—something drastic. For of all the peculiar mispronunciations his fledglings inflicted upon the English language, their blithe replacement of "v"s with "w"s and "w"s with "v"s was perhaps the most unnerving.

Mr. Parkhill realized that for some of his students, the speech habits of a lifetime were almost impossible to change: for instance, Mr. Kaplan said "fad" when he meant "fed" and "dad" when he meant "dead." He said "bad" when he meant "bed," but "bet" when he meant "bat." He used "full" when he meant "fool," and "pool" when he meant "pull." What particularly perplexed Mr. Parkhill was why Mr. Kaplan persisted in exchanging vowels *each of which he could enunciate with ease*. It was baffling.

Mr. Parkhill could understand the complex reasons for the wayward pronunciation of immigrants; after all, his students were adults, adults whose lips, tongues, teeth and larynxes had long been molded to vocalize their native phonemes. Such habitual reflexes, even the most tenacious teacher could rarely change, only regret.

Nor was Mr. Kaplan the worst offender. Take a line Mr. Pinsky had recently uttered: "He felt a pain in his hat."

That was improper dentalization; Mr. Pinsky simply let his tongue linger on his central incisors for a "t" instead of snapping right back for a "d." Or consider the speech habits which mangled so straightforward a monosyllable as "six" into:

| | |
|---|---|
| "seeks" | (Mr. Trabish) |
| "zix" | (Mr. Schmitt) |
| "sex" | (Miss Tarnova) |

Sometimes Mr. Parkhill wondered whether Miss Tarnova's pronunciation was rooted in her libido rather than her Russian.

Mr. Parkhill felt the most profound sympathy for refugees who had to reshape their lives, even more than their speech, in a new land, a land where, to their preconditioned ears, butter is spread on "brat," corn is eaten on the "cop," potato chips are picked out of a "back," and "coughing cake" is found in any decent bakery. Why, in one recent oration, Mr. Kaplan had praised a radio operetta he rashly called "Madman Butterfly"; worse, he had named the creators of that masterpiece as two Englishmen named "Gilbert and Solomon." And in an exercise on proper nouns, Mr. Kaplan had stated that Washington's Farewell Address was—Mount Vernon.

But sympathy is no substitute for pedagogy: Mr. Parkhill's task was to teach, not commiserate. He often told himself that the road to learning is harder for the pupil than the preceptor—for the latter is doubly rewarded: *Doce ut discas!* "Teach that you may learn." How true that was; and how it fortified one's strength in the trying hours.

Take the fricative spirants. What difficulties Mr. Parkhill had suffered because of fricative spirants! His classroom was a very charnel house of mismouthed "f"s and "v"s ("Vrankly, I lof to eat vish") and sometimes the room sounded beset by a blizzard of transposed "s"s and "z"s.

67

("Zelma broke the sipper on her zkirt.")

Or take the maddening "th." Mr. Parkhill often marveled over what happened when a student failed to respect the tiny but *enormous* difference between the "th" of "this" and the "th" of "throw." That might seem academic to people not engaged in teaching English; but it meant that pupils often converted a choice ("either") into an anesthetic ("ether").

Students from Germany practically wore their tongues out trying to pronounce that voiced fricative; yet, after months of effort, Mr. Schmitt had to settle for "Zanks" whenever he wanted to say "Thanks," and Mr. Finsterwald "truce" when what the poor man meant was "truth."

There was no end to the troubles hidden in the hard-hearted fricatives. Why, years ago a Mrs. Freda Gottschalk had electrified the class by confessing that she liked movie scenes in which the actors kissed mice. That, at least, is what it sounded like, and what precipitated a furious argument. The wrangling ended only when an alert student exclaimed, "She likes to see them kiss the *mouth,* not the 'mouse'!"

Or take the forward or trilled "r" as against the throat-born "r." (Plaut and Samish were particularly shrewd about that.) The voicing of "roar" or "rare" is child's play to those who have heard English spoken since their childhood; but had that childhood been spent in Budapest or Odessa, say, the "r"s would sound like gargling. (For fully four weeks after she had entered his fold, Mr. Parkhill thought Mrs. Moskowitz had a speech defect, when she was simply stranded at a phonetic frontier.)

Students from Cuba or Brazil *sang* rather than spoke English, Mr. Parkhill often said. They delivered a sentence in most melodious cadence: "I *go* to *store* to buy coff*ee*." The charming lilt was soothing to the ear, but fouled-up the code of comprehension.

Hispanic students said "thees" for "this" and "Djou" for "you." A Mrs. Rodriguez (or a Mr. Perez) would probably never learn how to pronounce "just" except as "zhust."

One night, a newcomer from Venezuela had held the class spellbound with his tale of a fortune-teller on a ship at sea—concluding, "No one did know where thees ztrange dark womon was come from."

The class was dumbfounded, until Mr. Parkhill cried: "Gypsy! *That's* what you meant. Not 'shipasy'!"

Yes, there was no end to the changes which the children of foreign cultures could ring on English. Mr. Parkhill had never forgotten Cornelius Hoogenhagen, from Holland, who simply could not vocalize the name of his adopted country in any way but "Unide Sdades." All of Mr. Parkhill's ingenuity failed to lure Mr. Hoogenhagen into relinquishing his native, sacred "d"s. He remained glued to "died" for "tide" and "delighded" for "delighted." Mr. Parkhill knew *Fortuna fortibus favet*—but not in pronunciation.

Another term, Mr. Parkhill had had to cope with Miss Antoinette Duvrier, who nearly went crazy trying to capture the lawless stresses of English words. Miss Duvrier could not *believe* the difference between "*ad*dress" as a noun and "ad*dress*" as a verb; she went blind before the chasm that separated "*in*sult" from "in*sult*"; and she virtually turned to putty the night Mr. Parkhill tried to teach her the important distinction between "*con*vict" and "con*vict*."

Miss Duvrier did not return to the class for a week. When she did, Mr. Parkhill was so pleased that he promptly gave the class a little exercise in shifting stresses: "*pro*test"—"pro*test*" ... "*reb*el"—"re*bel*" ... "*des*-ert—de*sert*." Whereupon Miss Duvrier picked up her reticule and left the room. Rumor had it that she had moved to Quebec.

Sometimes, Mr. Parkhill felt like Sisyphus; often he could not make up his mind *where* to concentrate his instruction; but he was verging more and more to the view that it was the vampire "v" and the waffled "w" which presented the most immediate challenge to his ingenuity.

During one recess, Mr. Parkhill sought the advice of Miss Higby in the faculty lounge. Miss Higby, who was a veteran of adult education, looked considerably younger than her years. Her complexion was fair, her cheeks pink, and the hair coiled upon her head was strawberry. Miss Higby was a teacher of unflinching temperament. She snapped out her sentences with the rapidity of a machine gun. Mr. Parkhill often envied Miss Higby her fearlessness, though he was sometimes troubled by her certitude.

"Miss Higby," Mr. Parkhill had come right out and said, "I am quite concerned about 'v's and 'w's!"

Without a second's hesitation Miss Higby proclaimed that no speech imperfection had given *her* so many sleepless hours as "the voiced fricative and labiodental consonant." (She was an M.A. from Teachers College.)

"My students just don't seem to be *interested* in altering their 'w's," frowned Mr. Parkhill.

"Nor their 'v's, Mr. Parkhill. Let's not gloss over those 'v's!"

"Oh, I *don't,*" said Mr. Parkhill.

Miss Higby tapped her temple. "Drill!"

"I beg your pardon."

"I said, 'Drill.'. . . Drill, drill, drill! That's the only way to cure lazy lips and stamp out careless habits!"

Mr. Parkhill adjusted his glasses. The last time he had tried a rigorous drill, in an exercise on hyphenated words ("hodge-podge," "helter-skelter"), Miss Kipnis had come up with "Willy and Nelly" (for "willy-nilly"), whereas Mr. Finsterwald had contributed "tops and turkey" (for "topsy-turvy").

"In any case," bristled Miss Higby, looking Mr. Parkhill straight in the eye, "their 'v's and 'w's should be improved, if not mastered, before you promote them to my grade!"

There was no mistaking her innuendo.

"Oh, I agree," said Mr. Parkhill. "I just wonder *how* one can—" The bell summoned them back to their duties before Mr. Parkhill could conclude, "—teach old dogs new tricks."

As he was entering his classroom, Miss Higby sang out from her own doorway: "Drill! *Drill!*"

"Thank you," said Mr. Parkhill. He wished Miss Higby would be a bit less militant about things. Her hair, at such times, seemed on fire.

Mr. Parkhill did not by nature like to discipline others; but once his sense of responsibility dictated a course of action, there were no bounds to his perseverance. The very next time an opportunity arose to grab the enunciation of "v"s and "w"s by the horns, Mr. Parkhill did not sidestep it.

During an exercise on vocabulary, Mr. Kaplan, asked to give a sentence containing the word "value," replied, "Vell, ven ve walue a t'ing, ve are villink to—"

"*Mr.* Kaplan!"

Mr. Kaplan stopped dead in his tracks. "I didn't findish."

"You didn't 'fin*ish*,' not 'fin*d*ish.' I want to comment upon your enunciation."

A guard reported for duty in Mr. Kaplan's left eye.

"Your 'v's and 'w's, Mr. Kaplan. You did not pronounce one of them correctly!"

"Not *vun?*"

"Not *one,*" winced Mr. Parkhill.

Mr. Kaplan simulated an attack of asthma.

"What *you* said was something like this." Mr. Parkhill cleared his throat. "'Ven *v*e *w*alue a thing, *v*e are *v*ill—'

and so on. You pronounced each 'w' as if it is a 'v,' and the 'v' as if it is a 'w'!"

Not with gloom or rue did Hyman Kaplan accept this reprimand. Instead, he sighed sheepishly, "Mine dobble-yous is tarrible, Mr. Pockheel, an' mine 'v's is a shame. Still, I'll try to awoid mistakes—"

" 'A*void*! There it is again!"

Mr. Kaplan recoiled. "I'm gaddink voise an' voise."

" '*W*orse and *w*orse!' " exclaimed Mr. Parkhill, a tinge of desperation in his tone. (He saw no point in confronting "gaddink" at a time like this.) "Class, do you see what I mean?"

The class displayed no doubts whatsoever about what Mr. Parkhill meant.

"Kaplen toins everything opside-don!" declared bald Bloom.

"Kaplin, give an inch!" begged Mrs. Shimmelfarb.

"This mon, this mon," croaked Olga Tarnova.

"Mr. Kaplan is not the only student," added Mr. Parkhill, "who commits this error . . ."

"By me is a 'v' like a knife in de mout," confessed Mrs. Yanoff.

"*Kill* me and I couldn't pronounce a 'w'!" proclaimed Wolfgang Schmitt. "In Cherman, ve alvays say 'v' vhen is printed 'w'!"

"So go beck to Joiminy," suggested Mr. Kaplan.

"Now, now." Mr. Parkhill tapped the desk with his pointer. "I know it seems difficult, but each of you really *can* conquer the—er—'v'-'w' habit. Even if you enunciate other consonants correctly, you—"

"What's 'consoments'?" asked Mr. Matsoukas.

Mr. Parkhill studied his knuckles. "Mr. Matsoukas, don't you remember our lesson on vowels and consonants?"

"No."

"Well'—Mr. Parkhill debated his next move—"we

haven't time to go into it thoroughly again, Mr. Matsoukas, but just to touch on the highlights: 'a,' 'e,' 'i,' 'o,' 'u,' and sometimes 'y' are vowels. All the other letters in our alphabet are called *con*-so-nants."

"I thought consoment is a soup," scowled the waiter from Athens.

"That's 'con*sommé,'* Mr. Matsoukas! Do you see how important pronunciation is?"

"Eesn't consonants what you have in a frand?" inquired Vincente Perez.

"That's 'con*fi*dence,' Mr. Perez! . . . Returning to 'v' and 'w,' we *must* train our lips to distinguish one from the other!"

"I know," mumbled Mrs. Tomasic—who, as it happened, never used "v"s for "w"s, only "w"s for "v"s. ("I will learn with wim and wigor," that Croatian once promised.)

"To me are 'w's like teffy-epples," grieved Mr. Vinograd.

Mrs. Moskowitz's "Oy!" conveyed an omnibus confession of fricative sins.

"Mine Gott!" Mr. Kaplan could contain himself no longer. "You vill all give Mr. Pockheel hot-failer!"

" '*W*ill,' not '*v*ill.' "

"*I* never say 'vill,' " smirked Mr. Finsterwald, "day or night."

"You hear how you slip?!" retorted Mr. Kaplan.

"Class, there is no reason to quarrel! Now, please. Watch my lips." Mr. Parkhill wet his lips. "First, I shall pronounce the 'v' sound." He opened his mouth, put his upper teeth on and overlapping his lower lip, took a deep breath, and was just about to emit a vivid "vvvvvv" when a sneeze from Mr. Scymczak shattered the spell.

Mr. Parkhill closed his mouth.

" 'Scooz," mumbled Mr. Scymczak miserably.

"Again, class. Notice: I place my upper teeth"—he tapped his upper teeth—"on my lower lip"—he tapped his lower lip—"and *push* my breath out to—"

"*Kachoo!*" sneezed poor Scymczak again.

Mr. Parkhill forced a smile onto his lips. "Watch my teeth. Ready . . ."

"Skimzek, hold *beck!*" cried Mr. Kaplan.

Mr. Parkhill turned to the blackboard. Perhaps it would be wiser to start with the "w" sound. He printed:

WE

" 'We,' " said Mr. Parkhill. "To pronounce this *very* common word, I round my lips this way"—he rounded his lips into a zero—"and say 'ooo.' O*oooo* . . ."

The class was bewitched.

"Will you all do that, please? Everyone. Round lips . . ." Thirty-odd students, puckering sixty-odd lips to encirculate thirty-odd mouths, looked as if they had swallowed alum. "Now, *without moving your lips,* simply expel your breath—'oooo'!"

Not a single lip moved as a ghostly "Ooooooo . . ." moaned through the room.

"Good! Now I shall say 'eeee.' Watch, please." Mr. Parkhill drew his lips far apart, clenched his teeth, and said, "Eeee . . . *eeee* . . . Class?"

The beginners' grade bared their teeth and blew forth a mistral of "Eeeee"s.

"Splendid!" said Mr. Parkhill. "Let's take the 'oooo' again. Round mouths . . . firm lips . . . expel. . . ."

"*Oooo,*" crooned the resolute chorus.

"Excellent. Now—lips apart, teeth together . . ."

"*Eeeee* . . ." keened the ardent scholars.

"Perfect!" smiled Mr. Parkhill. "Now let's put the two sounds *side by side*—this way." Mr. Parkhill rounded his lips. " 'Oooo.' " He bared his teeth. " 'Eeee.' "

They echoed: "Ooooo. . . . Eeeee . . . !"

"And *now,*" said Mr. Parkhill eagerly, "we put the two sounds closer, thus: 'Oooo-eee.' "

*"Oooo-ee ee!"*

"And if we *join* the two sounds, this way—'oo-ee,' 'oo-ee' . . ." his legion quivered with excitement "—we will pronounce a perfect 'WE'!"

"We!"

"We!"

"We!"

The first person plural whirled around the walls as if the celebrants were on a merry-go-round.

"Horrah!"

"I did it!"

"Me, too!"

"You *hoid?!*"

They were beside themselves—grinning, chortling, reeling on the heights of Parnassus. For they had, *mirabile dictu,* pronounced perfect "w"s. They had wrung the baffling and elusive secret from the voiced labial open consonant, which need never again strike terror in their hearts.

Mr. Parkhill was delighted, visibly, unashamedly delighted. "Again! *'We.'*"

"Oo-*ee!*" sang Miss Mitnick.

"Oo-ee . . . oo-*ee!*" wheed Oscar Trabish, as if it were New Year's Eve.

"Fine!" exclaimed Mr. Parkhill.

"W*ohn*derful," crooned Miss Tarnova.

"Look, look," cried Mr. Pinsky. *"Ooee, oo ee!"*

"Mr. Pockheel is a ginius!" rhapsodized Mr. Kaplan. "A regular ginius!"

"And again," called Mr. Parkhill. "Please face each other, so that you can *see* how it is done."

All through that happy chamber, students faced each other, rounding their lips, baring their teeth, pronouncing mellifluous "ooo-ee"s.

"Excellent, class! Perfect. You *see* how simple it is? Now, the very same use of your lips and teeth will pronounce perfect 'w's in *any* word!" He printed

on the board. "The same way, class. First, 'ooo' . . . then 'er.'
Then together, 'ooo-*er*'—'*ooo*-er'—which becomes 'were'!
All together . . . 'Ooo-er'—'were'!"

"Ooooo-*er*," came one great gust. "Were!"

"Ooooo-*ait*," called Mr. Parkhill. "Wait!"

"Ooooo-ait. *Wait!*"

"Ooooo-ish. *Wish.*"

"Ooooo-ish," they echoed, *"wish!"*

"Will . . . warm . . . woman . . ."

The "w"s rolled out in euphonious rondo.

"Want . . . winter . . . wake . . ."

Strong "Ooooo"s began each word; teeth flashed as lips
flew back to send another word starting with "w" winging
toward the stars.

"Now, let's try a whole sentence!" Mr. Parkhill's chalk
flashed across the board. The first part of the sentence he
devised was a stab in the dark, but the second was sheer
inspiration:

While we were waiting with William West, we were wondering where Walter White was.

"Ees plenty 'w's!" exclaimed Mr. Perez, who tended to be
literal-minded.

"Planty?" cried Mr. Kaplan. "Ha! Peratz, is *all* dobble-
yous! If Mr. Pockheel gives dobble-yous, he gives *dobble-
yous!*"

"Oy," faltered Mrs. Moskowitz.

Mr. Parkhill wiggled his pointer cheerfully. "You'll see
how simple it is to pronounce that sentence! Take it slowly.
Miss Kipnis."

Miss Kipnis rose, swallowed, reconnoitered the sentence
sprayed with "w"s like a scout expert in detecting am-
bushes, then, as Mr. Parkhill's pointer touched each word,

maneuvered her mouth around the fourteen "w"s ("Oo-ile oo-ee oo-ere oo-aiting oo-ith oo-illiam—") with not a single blunder.

"Congradjulations, Cookie!" cried Mrs. Shimmelfarb.

"T'ree chiss fa Kipnis!" exulted Mr. Kaplan.

*"Splen*did!" smiled Mr. Parkhill. "Next—" Mr. Kaplan was waving his hand furiously. "Miss Tarnova."

Miss Tarnova stood up, dabbing her perfumed handkerchief at her feverish lips, surveying the fearful stretches of "While we were waiting with William West, we were wondering where Walter White was," and bravely plunged forth. On the sixth "w" she stammered; on the ninth she turned pale; on the eleventh "w" she gulped; on the thirteenth she wailed, "No more! I go later."

Mr. Kaplan blared a call to the colors: "Tarnova, don't give op de sheep! Remamber Kipnis!"

Miss Tarnova fluttered her lashes, sniffed at a scent from Araby, rounded her mouth, and corraled the last "w" in that resplendent sentence.

*"Ex*cellent!" exclaimed Mr. Parkhill.

"Hau Kay," conceded Hyman Kaplan. (Olga Tarnova did not deserve "t'ree chiss": she had shown cowardice under fire.)

"Next—" Mr. Parkhill glanced around the room.

Everyone wanted to be next, their waving hands a veritable field of wheat in a wind.

"Er—"

Mr. Kaplan's hand was wig-wagging like a signal at a railway crossing. "Mr. Pockheel! Mr. Pockheel!" The man looked as if he would burst right there and then if denied his moment in the sun.

"Mr. Kaplan . . ."

Up rose the complete semaphore. "Hau *boy!*"

"Mr. Kaplan," Mr. Parkhill said earnestly, "be careful. Speak slowly. And remember, keep those lips round!"

"Arond itch dobble-you my mot is goink to make a detour! 'Oooooo' den 'eeee' . . . Hau Kay!" He flung his head back and charged. "Ooooo-ile! Ooooo-ee! Ooooo-ere! Ooooo-aiting . . ." The class was on the edge of their chairs. "Ooooo-ith ooooo-illiam ooooo-est—"

"Good, Mr. Kaplan!"

"—oo-ee ooo-ere ooo-ondering ooo-here ooo-alter ooo-ite ooo-as!"

"Perfect, Mr. Kaplan!"

*"Bella, bella!"*

Mr. Pinsky slapped both cheeks in homage, with a triumphant "Pssh!" thrown in for good measure.

"You see, class?" Mr. Parkhill laughed. "That's all there is to it! Now, if you will only *practice*—drill, drill, drill—"

"Prectice?" Mr. Kaplan's voice rang out. "Fromm nah on, ve vill voik vit dobble-yous till ve vouldn't iven vhisper vun void vitout—"

Mr. Parkhill did not hear the rest of that gallant pledge. Mr. Parkhill did not even see Mr. Kaplan. A black curtain had dropped over his eyeballs.

## MR. K·A·P·L·A·N
## AND THE HOBO

Despite Mr. Kaplan's distressing diction, his wayward grammar, his outlandish spelling, Mr. Parkhill was determined to treat him exactly as he treated every other pupil. Just because Mr. Kaplan referred to rubber heels as "robber hills," or transformed a pencil sharpener into a "pantsil chopner," was no reason to deny him equal time in class activities. (Mr. Parkhill's resolution *had* weakened a bit when Mr. Kaplan gave the opposite of "inhale" as "dead.")

Now Mr. Kaplan stood at the front of the room, right next to Mr. Parkhill's desk, smiling, primed to address his colleagues (whom he somehow treated as disciples) for three minutes of Recitation and Speech. (It often amazed Mr. Parkhill that three minutes could be so long.)

"Please speak slowly," said Mr. Parkhill. "Remember, it isn't how fast you talk, Mr. Kaplan, or—how much you crowd into your recitation. . . . Strive for accuracy, simplicity, directness. And enunciate as distinctly as possible."

The beam on the face of the cherub broadened.

"And watch your 'e's and 'a's! You tend to use one for the other quite—er—carelessly."

"I'll be so careful, Mr. Pockheel," the champing novice promised, "you'll positively be soprize!"

" 'Surprised,' Mr. Kaplan. . . . And, class, feel free to interrupt, if you have a correction, at any time." Allowing the class to cut in on a speaker had proved a real boon to Recitation and Speech. It not only kept the listeners on their toes; it made the reciters particularly careful. There was, after all, a certain stigma attached to being corrected by a student, instead of by Mr. Parkhill. "Very well, Mr. Kaplan. You may begin."

Pride stiffened Mr. Kaplan's stance, nobility suffused his demeanor. Mr. Kaplan loved to recite. He loved to write his homework on the board. In fact, he loved any chance to be the center of attention. Now he narrowed his eyes, shot his cuffs, and gazed into the empyrean. "Ladies an' gantleman —I s'pose dat's how I should aupen op—"

" 'Open up,' " said Mr. Parkhill.

"Open up," agreed Mr. Kaplan. He waved a gesture worthy of a cardinal. "In mine spitch tonight, becawss it's Rasitation an' Spitch time—"

" 'Speech,' Mr. Kaplan," Mr. Parkhill interpolated. "And 'my speech,' not 'mine' speech."

"So I'll talk about mine—no—my vacation!"

Mr. Parkhill, pleased, nodded.

Mr. Kaplan, delighted, nodded back. "So is de name fromm my speeech: 'My Hobo.' My hobo is—"

"Your what?" gaped Fanny Gidwitz.

"My hobo."

"No such woid!" shouted Mr. Bloom. (Whenever Norman Bloom sensed a departure from the orthodox, he charged that there was "no such woid.")

"No?" murmured Mr. Kaplan. "Maybe you positif?"

"There is such a word, Mr. Bloom," Mr. Parkhill put in hastily, "but, Mr. Kaplan, are you sure the word you mean is—uh—'hobo'?"

"Aha! So dere is soch a void!" Mr. Kaplan shriveled Mr. Bloom with scorn. "Vell, I t'ink I minn 'hobo,' Mr. Pockheel. My hobo is hikink—hikink in de voods, on de heels,

80

op an' don montains, all kinds hikink. Vhenever is a fine day, mit sonshinink—"

"He means 'hobby'!" exclaimed Miss Mitnick.

"Hobby?" yawned Oscar Trabish, awakening from his customary doze.

"So I'll say 'hobby.'" Mr. Kaplan acknowledged the emendation with a generous inclination of the head. "Vun point for Mitnick." He braced his shoulders. "De sky! De sonn! De moon! De stoss!—"

"'Stars'!"

"De clods! De frash air in de longs! De gress onder de fit! De sonds from beauriful boids—"

"'Beautiful birds,'" Mr. Parkhill cut in anxiously. "And it's 'sounds,' not 'sonds.'"

"—de sounds from beautiful birds, and bees, an' gless hoppers—all, all are pot fromm de vunderful vunders fromm Netcher!"

"'Nature,'" pouted Miss Valuskas.

"'Wonders' not 'vunders,'" sulked Vincente Perez.

"'Grasshoppers,' not 'glass' hoppers," gibed Mr. Marcus.

These petty alterations did not deter Hyman Kaplan. "An' do ve humans rilly appreciate? Are ve taking edwantage? Ha! No!" (Miss Mitnick, at whom the bard was glaring as if she were personally responsible for man's indifference to the out-of-doors, lowered her head.) "Dat's vhy I'm making such a hobby fromm hiking . . . Ladies an' gantleman! Have you vun an' all, or even saparate, falt in your soul dose trees, dose boids, de gress, de bloomers, de—"

Titters from two ladies and one outraged "Bloomers?!" forced Mr. Kaplan to halt, hand arrested in midair.

Mr. Parkhill cleared his throat. "What word are you using, Mr. Kap—?"

"All kinds."

"But you used one word—"

" 'Bloomers!' " blurted Mrs. Moskowitz. "That woid ain't nice in mixed company! Also bloomers come from ladies' stores, not nature!" As a matron, Mrs. Moskowitz could speak out where maidens of the class felt too genteel to object.

"I think he means 'flowers,' " Miss Mitnick shyly ventured.

"Don't mix op two languages, Keplan!" blared Mr. Blattberg, swinging his vest chain, from which his grandson's baby tooth dangled.

Mr. Parkhill, who had thought that "bloomers" came from a misconstruction of "to bloom," suddenly realized that *Blumen* were flowers in Mr. Kaplan's native tongue.

"So podden me, Moskovitz, t'anks a million, Mitnick, an' I take beck 'bloomers,' Blettboig, and put in 'flars.' "

" 'Fl*ow*ers,' " sighed Mr. Parkhill.

"I love dem! I also love to breed frash air. An' I *love* to hear de leetle boids sinking—"

" '*Singing!*' You *must* watch your 'k's and 'g's."

" '*Sink*ing' boids?" jeered Norman Bloom. "Kaplen, boids are not *fish!*"

The caustic thrust did not trouble the troubadour. "An' ven dose boids are sin*ging*, den is Mama Netcher commink ot in all kinds gorgeous!"

Mr. Parkhill rubbed his temples. *Epea pteroenta:* winged words—but on such ailing wings . . .

"Lest veek, I took my vife ot to de contry. I said, 'Sarah, you should take a vacation. Just slip, eat, valk aron' in Netcher. Stay in bad how late you vant itch mornink.' "

" '*Ea*ch morning.' "

"But my vife! Did she slapt late? No. Did she valk aron'? Saldom. Who ken change de life's times hebits of a poisson vun-two-tree? . . . Avery mornink my Sarah got op six o'clock, no matter vhat time it vas."

An explosion rocked the hall of learning.

"Mistake!"

"Mish-mosh!"

"Cuckoo!"

"I'll *die!*"

"Class . . . *class!*" pleaded Mr. Parkhill. "We *must* restrain ourselves! If you have a correction—yes, Miss Mitnick?"

Flushed but firm, Rose Mitnick responded, "How can Mr. Kaplan say Mrs. Kaplan got up every morning at six o'clock *'no matter what time it was'?*"

Laughter shook the faded walls.

"You right, Miss Mitnick!"

"Whoever heard such a silly?"

"With this mon, many mistakes are as sand on a bitch," Olga Tarnova gloated.

"Tarnova," lofty Kaplan inquired, "are you complainink or explainink?"

"Koplin!" railed Gus Matsoukas. "You should give *thanks* to Miss Mitnick!"

"I'll send her a talagram."

"Miss Tarnova iss right!" howled Wolfgang Schmitt.

"So give her a madel."

"Class—"

"Give an *inch,* Mr. Kaplen," wailed Bessie Shimmelfarb. "Give an *inch.*"

"I'm making a speech, not a ruler," rejoined the purist.

"Class! Let us confine our attention to the point at issue. Mr. Kaplan, I—I'm sure you didn't quite mean what you said in your last passage."

"Vhich pot?"

"Miss Mitnick," said Mr. Parkhill, "please repeat your point."

"I said that giving the exact t-time, six o'clock," Miss Mitnick stammered, "and *then* saying 'no matter what time it is'—that's impossible!"

Mr. Kaplan surveyed Rose Mitnick from Olympus. "Maybe for *som* pipple, it's umpossible. But *my* vife voke op so oily in de mornink she got op six o'clock no matter vhat time it vas!"

Miss Mitnick's expression was heart-rending. "But, Mr. *Kap*lan, if—"

"Don't be a stubborn, Kaplen!" bellowed Mr. Bloom. "If it's six o'clock, you *do* know what time it is, no?! So how can you say—"

"Aha!" cried Mr. Kaplan. "You make de same mistake Mitnick! Pay batter attention to my *minnink*. My vife is fest aslip. It's six o'clock. Hau Kay. She gats op. So does *she know vhat time it is*? Vould *you* know it's six o'clock if *you* are fest aslip?!"

Mr. Bloom ranted, Miss Mitnick whimpered, Mr. Pinsky sang "Pssh!" and slapped his cheek in tribute to his idol.

"*Mr.* Kaplan!" Mr. Parkhill repressed his desperation. "You are evading the point. If you state the exact time, then it is simply incorrect to add 'no matter what time it was.' That is a flat contradiction!"

Mr. Kaplan's smile ossified for a second, then recovered its aplomb. "If it's a *conter*diction, it's not just a mistake. Bloom, do you onderstand dis important difference?"

Mr. Bloom protested such shameless sophistry. Miss Goldberg choked on a lozenge. Miss Mitnick bit both her lip and her pencil in frustration. (Poor Miss Mitnick: ever correct, never victorious.)

"Koplan," croaked Olga Tarnova. "They should sand you to Siberia!"

"Dis is not a class in geography," observed Mr. Kaplan.

"*Mr.* Kaplan!"

The orator had flown back into rhapsody: "How many you city pipple aver saw de son rizink on a fild? How many you children from Netcher smalled de frash gress in de mornink, all vet mit dues? How many—"

No one would ever know how many "how many"s Mr. Kaplan still had in reserve, because the bell pealed in the corridor. The Cicero of the beginners' grade froze, hands in midair.

"That's all for tonight," said Mr. Parkhill. Only strength of character made it possible for him to conceal his relief.

Mr. Kaplan bowed to the cold-heartedness of time. "So dat must be de and fromm de speech of Hyman Keplen!"

And Mr. Parkhill saw the name. It was absurd, of course, utterly preposterous; but through some peculiar transmutation of sound into sight, Mr. Parkhill seemed to behold the name of Mr. Kaplan just as Mr. Kaplan always printed it: H*Y*M*A*N  K*A*P*L*A*N. How could a man pronounce his name in red and blue and green?

Mr. Parkhill sat quite still, frowning his perplexity, as the class filed out.

# MR. K·A·P·L·A·N,
# EVER MAGNIFICENT

Only after considerable soul-searching, plus the encouragement of Miss Higby (who was, after all, a blooded veteran of adult education), did Mr. Parkhill decide to introduce the beginners' grade to a new subject: writing letters. No instruction, surely, was more likely to benefit his pupils, or be put to swifter use outside the schoolroom.

So, one pleasant evening, as the long twilight bathed the walls in saffron, Mr. Parkhill opened the session by explaining the proper form and structure of personal letters: where to write the home address, where to place the date, how to phrase the salutation, how to word the final greeting. Rarely had his flock been so attentive; never had they displayed such eagerness to explore new terrain.

Now, the first fruits of Mr. Parkhill's tutelage glowed on the blackboards. Six happy students had transcribed the assignment: "A letter to your husband or wife, a relative or friend." Miss Mitnick had composed an *excellent* letter (as Mr. Parkhill had been confident she would) inviting her sister to a surprise party for one Lily Edelcup. Mr. Bloom had written a cousin in Los Angeles, Calif., describing a memorable Sunday of fun and frolic at Coney Island. Mr. Trabish had written to a friend in "Grand Rabbits," Michigan. Mrs. Rodriguez had reported her impressions of a New York subway ride to her mother in San Juan: "fast, but hot, noise, speet, durt, crazy." Mrs. Moskowitz had lolled in sweet fantasy by pretending she was vacationing in an elegant hotel in "Miami, Floridal," and reminded her husband, back home in Brooklyn, to be sure "the pussy gets each morning frash milk." (Mrs. Moskowitz was so devoted to "the pussy" that she repeated the admonition four times, which left insufficient room for a description that could do justice to the scenic beauties of Miami.) Mr. Kaplan—as Mr. Parkhill scanned the last letter on the board, his larynx knotted.

"It's to mine brodder," Mr. Kaplan explained.

Mr. Parkhill nodded absently.

"He lives in Varsaw."

"Mmh."

"Maybe I should rid *alod* de ladder," its author delicately suggested.

" '*Let*ter,' Mr. Kaplan, not '*lad*der.' "

"Aha! So maybe I ken rid de *let*ter. . . ."

"N-no, I'm afraid we won't have enough time."

Mr. Kaplan sighed, lamenting the heartlessness of Father Time.

"Class, please study Mr. Kaplan's letter carefully. . . ."

From their oaken, one-armed chairs, the company of scholars focused fiercely on the blackboard. Miss Mitnick quickly began making notes. Mr. Blattberg looked offended. Mr. Pinsky feasted on his hero's creation, then slapped his cheeks with ecstatic "Tchk! Tchk!'s." Mr. Matsoukas, demoralized by Mr. Pinsky's adoration, leaned far forward, as if the decreasing of distance would sharpen his critical faculties. Mrs. Moskowitz cast not a glance at the board; instead, she fanned her cheeks, exhausted. (The vicarious excitements of that evening had been too much for Mrs. Moskowitz: an invitation to a surprise party, a thrilling day at Coney Island, a ride on the Far Rockaway subway—it had been a veritable Mardi Gras for Sadie Moskowitz.)

And Hyman Kaplan sat in his chair as if on a throne, his

countenance proud, his indulgence spacious, his modesty fraudulent. He conducted a sidelong surveillance of those privileged to behold his handiwork, then gazed brightly at Mr. Parkhill. . . . Anxious little lines had crept around Mr. Parkhill's face when he first had scanned Mr. Kaplan's letter; naked disbelief possessed the leader's countenance as he read the epistle again:

459 E 3 Str<br>
N.Y.<br>
New York

Octo. 10

HELLO MAX!!!

I should tell about mine progriss. In school I am fine. Making som mistakes, netcheral. Also doing the hardest xrcises like the best students the same. Som students is Blum, Moskowitz, Mitnick—no relation Mitnick in Warsaw.

Max! You should absolutel come to N.Y. and belong in mine school!

(It was at this point, envisaging another Mr. Kaplan in the beginners' grade, that dismay invaded Mr. Parkhill's eyes.)

Do you feeling fine? I suppose. Is all ok? You should begin right now learning about ok! In America you got to say ok all the time. Ok the wether, ok the Prazident, ok the bazeball, ok the foot we eat.

(At this point, consternation covered all of Mr. Parkhill's features.)

How is darling Annie? Long should she leave!
So long.
With all kinds entusiasm,

Your animated brother<br>
H*Y*M*I*E

Mr. Parkhill turned to his flock. He tried to clear his throat, but succeeded only in coughing. "Has—everyone finished reading?"

The heads bobbed up and down like eager robins. That, at least, was encouraging. But the whispered chortles and mordant leers, the sly exchange of winks and grins and giggles, augured neither moderation nor mercy in the discussion that loomed ahead.

"Let us begin. One at a time, please. Who would like to start?"

The air turned into a palisade: pens, pencils, rulers, hands, fingers sprang up, and even a comb, swinging.

"Er—Mrs. Tomasic."

"Shouldn't 'N.Y.' be *after* 'New York'?" Mrs. Tomasic blurted. "So 'New York' should be on top of?"

"Good!" cackled Mr. Marcus.

Mr. Parkhill made the change on the board. "Mr. Finsterwald?"

"In all places is 'mine' positively wrong!" proclaimed Karl Finsterwald. "It should be 'my,' 'my,' 'my'!"

"Bravo!" trilled Carmen Caravello.

"Quite right," said Mr. Parkhill. "Mr. Kaplan—this really applies to everyone—you *must* learn the basic and important difference between 'my' and 'mine.' 'My' is an adjective; 'mine' is a pronoun—and is *never* used with a following noun!" On the board he swiftly chalked:

This is my towel.

"That," said Mr. Parkhill, "uses 'my' as an adjective. *But—*" Beneath the sentence, which seemed to have hypnotized Mr. Scymczak, Mr. Parkhill wrote:

This towel is mine.

"Here, 'mine' obviously refers to 'my towel.' So the first sentence would be altogether wrong if it read: 'This is *mine* towel.' . . . Is that clear?"

"Poifick!" affirmed Mr. Kaplan.

"Is the same also true with 'his' and 'her'?" asked Miss Pomeranz.

"Well . . ." Mr. Parkhill paused unhappily. "The adjective 'his' may be used both ways." He wrote:

> This is his toothbrush.
> This toothbrush is his.

"How*ever,* in the case of the pronoun 'her,' we have an unusual case—"

"Ooy!" Mrs. Moskowitz's morale melted like butter the moment "unusual" or "exception to the rule" emerged from Mr. Parkhill's lips.

"—because 'her' . . ." Quickly Mr. Parkhill scribbled:

> Her hat is yellow.
> The yellow hat is hers.

"—becomes 'hers.' "

*"No sanse,"* mumbled Mr. Scymczak.

"It's really not difficult," said Mr. Parkhill, "once you learn a few—"

"English don't stond still!" mourned Olga Tarnova. "In Rossian—"

"To return to Mr. Kaplan's letter . . . Further corrections?"

" 'Progress' is not with 'i,' " declared Miss Mitnick, "but with *'e,'* and 'some' needs at the end an *'e.' "*

"Very good . . . Mrs. Yanoff?"

"From the spelling of 'absolutel' I could *die!"* exclaimed the lady in black.

"Why?"

"It's spelled bad."

"How should it be spelled?"

"I don't know."

"Som corractor," snapped Mr. Kaplan.

Mr. Parkhill emended the word in contention.

"Vhy 'exercise' hass no 'e' before 'x'?!" demanded Wolfgang Schmitt.

" 'Baseball' weeth a *z'?!*" Young Vincente Perez, a fleet shortstop, was outraged.

"Who puts a 'z' in 'president'?" bristled Miss Valuskas.

The corrections came fast and furious: the absurd spelling of "weather," the butchered abbreviation of "October," the erratic tenses of verbs, the flagrant distortion of "Are you feeling fine?" into *"Do* you feeling fine?"

"Keplan has crimitted so many mistakes," shouted Mr. Feigenbaum, "we could make a whole book examples wrong English from that letter!"

"It's a mish-mosh!" blustered Mr. Blattberg. "Every type, size and amont of!"

"Yos," rumbled Mr. Matsoukas. "Give exomples!"

Norman Bloom swooped in from the sidelines with examples. "Kaplen means 'Long should she *live'*—not 'Long should she *leave,'* which means 'Go away from here!' and is a tarrible way to talk about a sister-on-law!"

His cohorts gave Mr. Bloom an ovation.

"He even—*spelled—wrong—my—name!*" fumed Mr. Bloom, his indignation making it clear that this was the most intolerable of Mr. Kaplan's errors.

"Shame!" foamed Olga Tarnova. "To spell wrong a mon's name! Koplon, Koplon . . ."

"Is in my name double 'o,' not 'u'! I ain't like *som* Blooms!" With this restoration of the honor of the House of Bloom, its scion sneered at his nemesis.

"Goot fa you!" sang Mr. Kaplan, bewildering his adversaries. "Bloom, you gattink batter an' batter to spit so many mistakes."

91

" *'Spot'* so many mistakes!" exclaimed Mr. Parkhill.

Mr. Bloom's bald scalp prickled in confusion.

Mr. Kaplan half rose. "I give formal congradulation to Norman Bloom for his improvink in English!"

"That's nice," observed Mrs. Shimmelfarb.

" *'Nice?'* " retorted Mr. Pinsky. "Mr. Keplen is *big!* Only a big men edmits small mistakes!"

"For that Kaplin desoives credit," chimed in "Cookie" Kipnis.

Mr. Bloom looked flabbergasted. Mr. Kaplan's manly gesture was not pure gallantry, for it diverted attention from his blunders to Mr. Bloom's progress. In consequence, Mr. Bloom did not know whether to feel flattered or irate. Vanity squelched umbrage. "Thank you, Kaplen!"

"My plashure, Bloom," murmured Machiavelli.

Mr. Nathan burst into laughter.

Mr. Parkhill, realizing why the preceding fusillade had made no dent in Mr. Kaplan's self-esteem (the man had merely been busy loading his weapons), lowered his pointer. "Any more corrections?"

Miss Mitnick flushed. " 'N-e-t' in 'natural' should be 'n-a-t,' with no 'ch' and a 'u,' not an 'e.' And we eat *'food,'* not 'foot'!"

Mr. Blattberg shook with spring giggles. "A foot is for walking, not itting!"

"Also, a small 'ok' is wrong," continued the hawk-eyed damsel. "Should always be 'O.K.' with capitals and periods, because 'O.K.' is an abbreviation."

Mr. Kaplan fashioned the most debonair of smiles. (What was he planning now? Mr. Parkhill wondered.) "Good, Mitnick."

Strengthened by virtue, Miss Mitnick rode to an unseen abyss. "Finally, *three* exclamation points after 'Hello Max'?! You are wrong."

"Aha! . . . Vhy?"

"B-because one exclamation point is plenty!"

"Podden me, Mitnick," crooned Mr. Kaplan. "Your odder corractinks vere fine, Hau Kay—an' I minn Hau Kay mit capitals an' periods. But I soggest you riconsider your remocks abot t'ree haxclimation points. . . ."

"Mr. Kaplan," said Mr. Parkhill firmly, "Miss Mitnick is entirely right. If you feel that you *must* use an exclamation point"—he was guarding himself on all sides—"then one is certainly sufficient."

*"For de vay I'm fillink abot mine brodder?!"* In that deadly riposte, sublime in its simplicity, Mr. Kaplan virtually accused Miss Mitnick of (1) familial apathy, and (2) trying to undermine the powerful love between blood brothers.

"Not so fast, Kaplen!" Mr. Bloom rushed to Rose Mitnick's defense. *"Three* exclamation marks?!"

"Mex is my *favorite* brodder," declared Mr. Kaplan.

"I don't care if he's your favorite mother!" raged Mr. Bloom.

"My mother isn't 'he,' an' besites she ken't rid English."

"Red harring!" stormed Mr. Blattberg. "Get back to your brother—"

"For a favorite brodder you vant *vun leetle* haxclimation point?" Mr. Kaplan retorted. "Ha! Dat I give to *strengers!"*

Mr. Blattberg howled, Miss Mitnick whinnied, Mr. Bloom turned apoplectic, and Rochelle Goldberg swallowed two nougats.

"Class—"

"Keplen could be right!" opined Sam Pinsky. "A brother desoives more exclamation points than a stranger!"

"I agree," said Miss Gidwitz.

"Class—"

"Then how about the word 'entusiasm'?" Miss Mitnick protested. "It is spelled without 'h'! And is 'With all *kinds* enthusiasm' a way to end a letter?!"

"Vell," Mr. Kaplan admitted, "maybe 'entusiasm' is

spalled wronk; but not de vay I'm *us*ink it. Because *I* write to my brodder *mit real entusiasm!*"

The implication was clear: Rose Mitnick was one of those ingrates who, corrupted by the wealth of the New World, would let her brother starve overseas.

*"Mr.* Kaplan!" Mr. Parkhill could bear no more. "I—"

"I love my brother more than you!" charged Gus Matsoukas.

"So give him a samicolon," shrugged Mr. Kaplan.

"Kaplan, give an *inch!*" wailed Bessie Shimmelfarb. "Give an *inch!*"

He waved off an invisible mosquito.

"But, Mr. Kaplan—" Miss Mitnick tried one final plea for reason. "Take that word 'animated.' 'Your *animated* brother, Hymie?' Isn't *that* wrong?"

"Yes," said Mr. Parkhill flatly. " 'Animated' is quite out of place!"

Mr. Kaplan squinted sincerely. "I looked op dat void in de dictionary. It minns 'full of life.' Vell, I falt planty full of life vhen I was wridink to Mex."

Miss Mitnick collapsed.

"That is *not* the point," said Mr. Parkhill severely. "We say that someone has an animated manner, or we say, 'The music has an animated refrain.' But—"

Mr. Kaplan's orbs widened. "Ken't you fill enimated onless you play music?"

"—one just does not say 'your animated *brother*'!"

Applause rattled from the anti-Kaplan cabal; gloom enveloped Mr. Kaplan's grenadiers.

"There is a better word to convey your—feelings in your final greeting," Mr. Parkhill swiftly added. "How about— 'fond'? 'Your *fond* brother—er—Hyman'?" (His lips refused to form "Hymie.")

" 'Fond'?" Mr. Kaplan closed his eyes, referring this moot point to his Muse. " 'Fond' . . ." he whispered. " 'Your fond brodder, Hymie.' " He shook his head, all regret.

" 'Fond' is a fine void, Mr. Pockheel—but it don't have enough *fill*ink."

"Then what about 'dear'?! 'Your *dear* brother'—and so on."

Once more Mr. Kaplan went through the process of interior consultation. " 'Dear' . . . 'dear' . . . 'Your dear brodder, Hymie.' " He grimaced. " 'Dear' is too *common.* . . ."

"Then what about—"

"Aha!" cried Mr. Kaplan. "I got it! Fine! Poifick! *Soch* a void!" His smile could have lighted a village.

"Yes, Mr. Kaplan?"

"Give it," urged Shirley Ziev.

"Tell!" begged Sam Pinsky.

" 'Megnificent!' " said Hyman Kaplan.

The class sat dumfounded. " 'Your magnificent brother, Hymie.' " It was the stroke of a master.

All heads turned to Mr. Parkhill. He cleared his throat.

"N-no, Mr. Kaplan. I'm afraid 'magnificent' is entirely inappropriate."

The parting bell pealed down the hall. The beginners' grade rose as one, gathering up foolscap, notebooks, pencils, even as they affirmed their loyalties; some branded Mr. Kaplan a brazen "shop-shooter," others praised so inspired and independent a spirit. Nathan P. Nathan, who so loved life that he never took sides, soothed Miss Mitnick by laughing as he patted her hand. "It's only a lesson, Rose. Next time you'll trap him!"

The last to depart were Messrs. Pinsky and Kaplan.

"Keplen," grinned Mr. Pinsky. "Tonight, you vere tremandous! Where you hoid such a wonderful woid?"

" 'Megnificent,' " Mr. Kaplan savored the lilt of those syllables. "A *beautiful* void. . . ."

"Believe me!" burbled Mr. Pinsky. *"Splan*did. Onusul! But how you found it?"

"By *dip* tinking."

95

# 9

# THE NIGHT OF THE MAGI

When Mr. Parkhill noticed that Miss Mitnick, Mr. Bloom, and Mr. Kaplan were absent, and heard a mysterious humming beneath the ordinary sounds which preceded the start of a class session, he realized that it was indeed the last meeting of the year, and that Christmas was but a few days off.

Every grade in the American Night Preparatory School for Adults each year presented a Christmas gift to its teacher. By now, Mr. Parkhill was quite familiar with the ritual. Several nights ago, there must have been a concerted dunning of those who had not yet contributed to the collection. Now the Gift Committee was probably engaged in last-minute shopping in Mickey Goldstein's Arcade, debating the propriety of a pair of pajamas, examining the color combination of shirts and ties, arguing whether Mr. Parkhill, in his heart of hearts, would prefer fleece-lined slippers to onyx cuff links.

Mr. Parkhill cleared his throat. "We shall concentrate on spelling tonight."

The students smiled knowingly, stealing glances at the three empty chairs, exchanging sly nods and soft chuckles. Mrs. Moskowitz directed a question to Mrs. Tomasic, but Mr. Blattberg's fierce "Shah!" murdered the words on her very lips. Rochelle Goldberg reached for a chocolate, giggling, but swallowed the sound instead of the sweet the moment Mr. Perez shot her a scathing rebuke.

"We shall try to cover—forty words before recess!"

Not one stalwart flinched.

Mr. Parkhill always gave the class a brisk spelling drill during the last session before Christmas: that kept all the conspirators busy; it dampened their excitement over what would soon transpire; it involved no speeches or discussion during which the precious secret might be betrayed; above all, a spelling drill relieved Mr. Parkhill from employing a rash of ruses to conceal his embarrassment. "Is everyone ready?"

A chorus worthy of *Messiah* choraled assent.

"The first word is—'bananas.' "

Murmurs trailed off, smiles expired, as "bananas" sprouted their letters on the arms of the chairs.

"Romance . . ."

Pens scratched and pencils crunched as "romance" joined "bananas."

" 'Fought,' the past tense of 'fight' . . . *'fought.' "* Now all brows tightened (nothing so frustrated the fledglings as the gruesome coupling of "g" and "h") while the scholars wrestled with "fought."

"Groaning . . ." Mr. Parkhill heard himself sigh. The class seemed incomplete without its stellar student, Miss Mitnick, and bereaved without its unique one, Hyman Kaplan. (Mr. Kaplan had recently announced that Shakespeare's finest moments came in that immortal tale of star-crossed lovers, "A Room in Joliet.")

"Charming . . . horses . . ." Mr. Parkhill's mind was not really on charming horses. He could not help feeling uneasy as he envisaged what soon would occur. The moment the recess bell rang, the entire class would dash out the door. The committee would be waiting in the corridor. The class would cross-examine them so loudly that Mr. Parkhill would get a fairly good idea of what the present was. And as soon as the bell pealed its surcease, the throng would pour in from the corridor, faces flushed, eyes aglitter, surrounding one member of the committee (the one carrying the Christmas package) to conceal the fateful parcel from their master's view.

The class would come to order with untypical celerity. Then, just as Mr. Parkhill resumed the spelling lesson, the chairman would rise, apologize for interrupting, approach Mr. Parkhill's desk, place the package upon it, and blare out the well-prepared felicitations.

Mr. Parkhill would pretend to be overwhelmed by surprise; he would utter a few halting phrases. His flock would smile, grin, fidget until the bravest among them would exclaim, "Open it!" or "Look inside the present!" Whereupon, Mr. Parkhill would untie the elaborate ribbons, remove the wrapping from the box, lift the top, and —as his students burbled with pleasure—he would pluck the gift from its cradle, exclaiming "It's *beau*tiful!" or "I shall certainly put *this* to good use!" or (most popular of all) "It's just what I wanted!"

The class would burst into a squall of applause, to which he would respond with renewed thanks and a stronger counterfeit of spontaneous thanksgiving. (It was not always easy for Mr. Parkhill to carry off the feigned surprise; it was even harder for him to pretend he was bowled over by pleasure: One year the committee, chairmanned by Mr. David Natkowitz, had given him a porcelain nymph—a pixy executing a fandango despite the barometer in her right hand and the thermometer in her left.)

As Mr. Parkhill's remarks concluded, and the class's "Don't mention it!"'s and communal fervor trailed off, the spelling drill would resume and the session would drag on until the final bell.

"Accept . . ." called Mr. Parkhill. "Notice, please, the

word is *'acc*ept' . . . Not, *'ex*cept'; be careful everyone; listen to the difference: *ex*cept . . . 'Cucumber . . .' "

And after the final bell rang, the whole class would cry "Merry Christmas! Happy New Year!" and crowd around him with tremendous smiles to ask how he *really* liked the present, advising him that if it wasn't just right in size and color (if the gift was something to wear), or in shape and utility (if something to use), Mr. Parkhill could exchange it! He didn't *have* to abide by the committee's choice. He could exchange the present—for anything! That had been carefully arranged with Mickey Goldstein in person.

This was the ritual, fixed and unchanging, of the session before Christmas.

"Nervous . . . goose . . . violets . . ."

The hand on the wall clock crawled toward eight. Mr. Parkhill tried to keep his eyes away from the seats, so telling in their vacancy, of Miss Mitnick, Mr. Bloom, and Mr. Kaplan. In his mind's eye, he saw the three deputies in the last throes of decision in Mr. Goldstein's Arcade, torn by the competitive attractions of an electric clock, a cane, spats, a "lifetime fountain pen." Mr. Parkhill winced. Twice already had "lifetime" fountain pens been bestowed upon him, once with a "lifetime" propelling pencil to match. Mr. Parkhill had exchanged these indestructible gifts discreetly: once for a woolen vest, once for a fine pair of earmuffs. Mr. Parkhill hoped it wouldn't be a fountain pen.

Or a smoking jacket! He had never been able to understand why the committee, in his second semester at the A.N.P.S.A., had decided upon a smoking jacket. Mr. Parkhill did not smoke. He had exchanged it for a pair of fur-lined gloves. (That was when Mr. Goldstein told him that teachers were always changing the Christmas presents their classes gave them: "Why don't those dumbbells maybe ask a teacher some questions in advance they could

99

get a *hint* what that particular teacher really *wants?*" Mr. Goldstein had been quite indignant about such foolhardiness.)

"Pancakes . . . hospital . . . commi—" In the nick of time, as a dozen apprehensive faces popped up, Mr. Parkhill detoured disaster: "—*ssion.* Commission! . . ."

The clock ticked away.

Mr. Parkhill called off "Sardine . . . exquisite . . . palace" —and at long last the bell trilled intermission.

The class stampeded out of the room, Mr. Pinsky well in the lead. Their voices resounded in the corridor and floated through the open door. Nathan P. Nathan was playing a harmonica. Mr. Parkhill began to print "Bananas" on the blackboard; he would ask his pupils to correct their own papers after the recess. He tried to shut his ears to the babbling forum outside the door, but the voices chattered like shrill sparrows.

"Hollo, Mitnick!"

"Bloom, what you chose?"

"Ees eet for wear?"

"So what did you *gat,* Keplen? Tell!"

Mr. Parkhill heard Miss Mitnick's "We bought—" instantly squashed by Mr. Kaplan's stern "Mitnick! Don't say! Averybody comm *don* mit your voices. Titcher vill hear soch hollerink. Be soft! Qviet!" Mr. Kaplan was born to command.

"Did you bought a Tsheaffer's Fountain Pan Sat, guaranteet for life, like *I* said?" That was Mrs. Moskowitz. (Poor, dear Mrs. Moskowitz; she showed as little imagination in her benefactions as in her homework.)

"Moskovitz, mine *Gott!*" The stentor was Kaplan. "Vhy you don't use a lod spikker?! Cless, lat's go to de odder and fromm de hall!"

The voices of the beginners' grade dwindled as they marched to the "odder and" of the corridor, rather like the

100

chorus in *Aida* (which, in fact, Mr. Nathan was playing, off-key) vanishing into Pharaoh's wings.

Mr. Parkhill printed "Horses" on the board, then "Accept . . . Except," and he began to practice the murmur: "Thank you . . . all of you . . . It's just what I wanted!" Once he had forgotten to say "It's just what I wanted!" and Miss Helga Pedersen, chairman of the committee that year, had been hounded by her classmates well into the third week of January.

It seemed an hour before the gong summoned the scholars back to their quarters. They poured in *en masse*, restraining their excitement by straining their expressions, resuming their seats with simulated insipidity.

Mr. Parkhill, printing "Cucumber" on the board, did not turn to face his congregation. "Please compare your own spelling with mine—"

Came a heated whispering: "Stand *op*, Mitnick!" That was Mr. Kaplan. "You should stend op, too!"

"The *whole* committee," Mr. Bloom rasped.

Apparently Miss Mitnick, a gazelle choked with embarrassment, could not mobilize the fortitude to "stend op" with her comrades.

"A fine represantitif *you'll* gonna make!" frowned Mr. Kaplan. "You t'ink is for *my* sek I'm eskink? Mitnick, stend *op!*"

"I can't," whinnied Miss Mitnick.

Mr. Parkhill printed "Violets."

"Lest call!" barked Mr. Kaplan. "Come op mit me an' Bloom!"

The anguished maiden's eyes were glazing. Even Mr. Nathan's cheerful "Rosie!" fell on paralyzed ears.

"Class . . ." began Mr. Parkhill.

A clarion voice cut through the air. "Podden me, Mr. Pockheel!"

It had come.

"Er—yes?" Mr. Parkhill beheld Messrs. Bloom and Kaplan standing side by side in front of Miss Mitnick's chair. Each was holding one side of a long package, wrapped in green cellophane and tied with great red ribbons. A pair of tiny hands, their owner hidden behind the box, clutched the bottom of the offering.

"De hends is Mitnick," explained Mr. Kaplan.

Not for a second did Mr. Parkhill avert his gaze from the tableau. "Er—yes?"

"Lat go," Mr. Kaplan whispered.

The hands of Mitnick disappeared.

The diminished committee advanced with the parcel. Mr. Kaplan's smile was celestial; Mr. Bloom's nostrils quivered. Together, the staunch duo thrust the package toward Mr. Parkhill's chest as Mr. Kaplan proclaimed: "Mr. Pockheel, is mine beeg honor, as chairman fromm de Buyink-an'-Deliverink-to-You-a-Prazent Committee, to prezant you mit dis fine peckitch!"

Mr. Bloom dropped back two paces (it resembled the changing of the guard, so well had it been rehearsed) and stared into space.

Mr. Parkhill stammered, "Oh, *goodness*. Why, thank—" but Mr. Kaplan rode over his words: "Foist, I have to say a few voids!" He half turned to the audience. "Mitnick, *you still got time to join de committee!*"

The maiden was inert.

"She fainted!" cried Mrs. Yanoff.

This was not true.

"She is stage-fried!"

This, despite the solecism, was true.

Mr. Kaplan shook his head in disgust and re-faced Mr. Parkhill, smoothed a paper extracted from his pocket, and read: "To our dear titcher (dat's de beginnink): Ve are stendink on de edge of a beeg holiday. Ufcawss, is all kinds holidays in U.S.: holidays for politic, holidays for religious, an' *plain* holidays. In Fabruary, ve got Judge Vashington's boitday—a *fine* holiday. Also Abram Lincohen's, iven batter. In July comms, netcheral, Fort July, de boitday of America de beauriful.... Also ve have Labor Day, Denksgivink (for de Peelgrims), an' for victory in de Voild Vide Var, Armistress Day."

Mr. Parkhill studied his chalk. "Thank—"

"Make an *end* awreddy," growled Mr. Bloom.

Mr. Kaplan scorned impatience at such a moment. "But arond dis time year, ve have a *different* kind holiday, a spacial, movvellous time: Chrissmas. All hover de voild are pipple celebraking. Becauss for som pipple is Chrissmas like for *odder* pipple Chanukkah—de most secret holiday fromm de whole bunch."

(" 'Sacred,' Mr. Kaplan, *'sa*cred.' ")

"Ven ve valkink don de stritts an' is snow on de floor an' all kinds tarrible cold!" Mr. Kaplan's hand repelled winter's tribulations. "Ven ve see in all de chop-vindows dose trees mit rad an' grin laktric lights boinink ... Ven de time comms for tellink fancy-tales abot Sandy Clawss—"

(*"Fai*ry tales ...")

"—flyink don fromm de Naut Pole on rain-emimals, an' climbink don de jiminies mit stockings for all de lettle kits. Ven ve hear de beauriful t'oughts of de tree Vise Guys, chasink a star on de dasert to Bettelheim."

(*"Mis*ter Kaplan!")

"Ven pipple saying, 'Oh, Mary Chrissmas! Oh, Heppy Noo Yiss! Oh, bast regotts!'—den ve *all* got a varm fillink in de hot, for all humanity vhich should be brodders! Ve know *you* got de fillink, Mr. Pockheel; *I* got de fillink; Caravello, Matsoukas, iven Mitnick"—Mr. Kaplan was not one to let perfidy go unchastised—"got dat fillink!"

*"I* feel my feet dying," muttered Mr. Bloom.

"An' vat do ve call dis fillink?" cried Mr. Kaplan. "De Chrissmas Spirits."

(" 'Spir*it*,' Mr. Kaplan, 'spir—' ")

*"Now* I'll prezant de prazent."

The class leaned forward. Mr. Parkhill straightened his shoulders.

"Because you a foist-cless titcher, Mr. Pockheel, an' ve all oppreciate how you explain de hoddest pots gremmer, spallink, pernonciation, vhich ve know is planty hod to do mit greenhorns, ve all falt you should gat a semple of our —of our"—Mr. Kaplan turned his page over hastily—"Aha! —of our santimental! So in de name of de beginnis' grate of Amarican Night Priparatory School for Edults, I'm prezantink de soprize prazent to our vunderful titcher, lovely Mr. Pockheel!"

(" *'Beloved,'* Mr. Kaplan . . .")

A hush gripped the chamber.

Mr. Parkhill tried to say, "Thank you, Mr. Kaplan . . . Thank you, class . . ." but the phrases seemed so time-worn, so shorn of meaning, they stuck in his throat. Without a word, he untied the big red ribbon, unfolded the green cellophane wrapping, lifted the cover off the package, fumbled with the inner maze of wrapping. He raised the gift from the box. It was a smoking jacket. A black and gold smoking jacket. Black velvet, the lapels a lustrous gold. On the breast pocket, an exotic ideograph sparkled. And a dragon was embroidered all across the front and back; its tongue flickered across the sleeves.

"Horyantal style," Mr. Kaplan confided.

Mr. Parkhill coughed. The room seemed very warm. Mr. Bloom was peering over Mr. Kaplan's shoulder, mopping his bald head and clucking like a rooster. Mrs. Moskowitz sat stupefied. Moist-eyed Olga Tarnova moaned from the depths of one of her many passions.

"Th-thank you," Mr. Parkhill succeeded in stammering. "Thank you—all of you—very much."

Mr. Bloom blared, "Hold it op everyone should see!"

Mr. Kaplan turned on Mr. Bloom. *"I'm* de chairman!"
Rose Mitnick was bleating.

Miss Goldberg cracked a pistachio nut.

"I—I can't tell you how much I—appreciate your kindness." The dragon, Mr. Parkhill noted, had green eyes.

Mr. Kaplan beamed. "So plizz hold op de prazent all should see."

Mr. Parkhill raised high the jacket for all to behold. The symphony of admiring "Oh!"'s and "Ah!"'s was climaxed by Mr. Kaplan's ecstatic "My!"

"It's—beautiful," said Mr. Parkhill.

"Maybe you should toin arond de jecket," suggested Mr. Kaplan.

As Mr. Parkhill revolved the jacket slowly, the dragon writhed in the folds.

"A voik of art!" sang Mr. Pinsky.

"Maybe ve made a mistake?" whispered Hyman Kaplan.

"I beg your pardon?"

"Maybe you don't smoke. Mitnick vorried abot dat. But I sad, 'Uf *cawss* a ticher smokes. Not in cless, netcheral. At home. At least a *pipe!*' "

"No, no, you didn't make a mistake. I do—occasionally—smoke. A pipe!" Mr. Parkhill cleared his larynx. "Why—*it's just what I wanted!*"

The class burst into cheers.

"Hooray!" laughed Mr. Trabish.

"I knew it!" boomed Mr. Blattberg, whirling his grandson's tooth.

"Hoorah," growled Gus Matsoukas.

"Bravo!" chimed Miss Caravello.

"In Rossia we song in all the chaurches," droned Olga Tarnova. "On differont day but."

"Vear it in de bast of helt!!" cried Mr. Kaplan.

"Thank you, I will. Class, you have been most generous. Thank you."

105

"You welcome!" came the congregation's response.

It was over.

Mr. Parkhill started to fold the dragon back into its lair. Mr. Bloom marched to his seat, acknowledging the praises due a connoisseur who had participated in such a choice. But Mr. Kaplan stepped closer to Mr. Parkhill's desk.

"Er—thank you, Mr. Kaplan," said Mr. Parkhill.

The chairman of the committee shuffled his feet and craned his neck and—why, for the first time since Mr. Parkhill had known him, Mr. Kaplan was embarrassed.

"Is anything wrong?" asked Mr. Parkhill anxiously.

*Sotto voce,* so that no ears but Mr. Parkhill's could hear it, Mr. Kaplan said, "Maybe mine spitch vas too long, or too *formal.* But, Mr. Pockheel, avery void I sad came fromm below mine heart!"

For all the unorthodox English, thought Mr. Parkhill, Mr. Kaplan had spoken like one of the Magi.

# 10

## THE SUBSTITUTE

Sleet slithered down the windows. The room smelled of wet coats, drying above the radiators, and soaked hats and damp mufflers, dangling from pegs along the side wall, where many rubbers crouched and galoshes glared like brass-eyed gnomes. Dripping umbrellas, some open, some closed, were propped along the back wall, beneath the lithographs of Washington and Lincoln that flanked the forlorn panes.

It was a nasty night, a night of soaked shoes, raw throats, sniffles and snuffles and sudden sneezes. A fourth of the chairs were empty, their occupants at home. So was Mr. Parkhill.

At his desk and in his stead, a young Substitute, bubbling with missionary zeal (it was only the second time he had been summoned to "fill in" for an indisposed teacher), was addressing the beginners' grade.

Actually, the Substitute had taken his stand in *front* of Mr. Parkhill's desk. (Any graduate student in Education knows that standing in front of a desk creates a closer rapport than standing behind it; one is more effective, psychologically, posed before instead of behind the site of authority. As for sitting in the *chair* of the teacher for whom you are a proxy, that is "an insensitive beginning," Plaut and Samish warned the unwary, "for it converts the substitute into an usurper. To take command so brusquely is to offend some students' loyalty—and may even arouse the resentment of others."

Plaut and Samish had gone on, in their masterful chapter called "Emergency Pitfalls," to ordain:

> A desk is more than a desk. It is a lectern, a pulpit, even a dais. Let no teacher forget that if he adopts the demeanor of a judge, he transforms a classroom into a court—in which his comments become verdicts, his sentences *sentences*.

No one ever put that better.

"—and so, unfortunately, Mr. Parkhill shan't be with you tonight. But I shall do my best—"

"Teacher is sick?" gasped one woman.

"Mr. Parkheel is *home?*" gulped another.

"Lat's hope it's not seryous!" intoned the gentleman in the exact center of the front row.

"Oh, I'm sure it's nothing more than a cold." The Substitute spread an emollient smile.

"Vunderful!"

"Mr. Parkhill told me he will surely be back on Monday, Mr.—?"

"Keplen."

"—Mr. Kaplan."

"*Hy*man Keplen."

"Hyman Kaplan," the tutor echoed, examining this pupil with curiosity. He beheld a pleasant, plump gentleman with twinkling blue eyes, blondish hair, and an elfin, debonair manner. A debonair elf was something the young Substitute had never before encountered. And when the elf smiled, as he was doing now, he took on the radiance of a cherub.

Mr. Kaplan, for his part, was appraising Mr. Parkhill's replacement. "Should be taller," noted Mr. Kaplan (the young man *was* shorter than Mr. Parkhill), "and more skinny" (an odd cavil, considering the fact that Mr. Kaplan was considerably weightier), "an' he should at *list* have more hair on his chiks!" (*That* critique was valid, for the surrogate lacked hirsute jowls.)

"I can assure you all," the Substitute continued, "that Mr. Parkhill will rejoin you fit as a fiddle."

"Mr. Parkhall plays the *feedle?*" exclaimed a matron in black.

"No, no," the Substitute exclaimed. "That's just a way of saying he will come back in perfect health!"

"Ufcawss," said Mr. Kaplan.

"Aman," added a voice from the rear.

"That takes a load off!" declared a mustached male.

"Sir," the Substitute said at once, "I believe you mean 'That takes a load off *my mind*'!"

"He sad 'Sir' to a *student?*" a swarthy brunette asked her neighbor.

"Vary polite," the neighbor whispered back.

"Well, class, suppose we follow Mr. Parkhill's schedule tonight and—"

Up rose the hand of Mr. Kaplan.

"Yes?"

"Podden me, but ken ve know *your* name?"

The Substitute flushed boyishly. "Oh, I *am* sorry. My name is Mr. Jennings."

From the expression on Mr. Kaplan's face, the name belonged to a Choctaw. *"Chann*ink?" he echoed.

"No, no. *Jen*nings." The instructor stepped to the blackboard; his chalk sped through J-E-N-N-I-N-G-S.

"Aha!" Mr. Kaplan nodded sagely. *"Chenn*ink! I t'ought you said *'Chann*ink!' "

"N-no, sir, I'm quite sure I said *'Jen*nings.' "

"Mr. Jenninks," announced Mr. Kaplan, "valcome! An' don't be noivous."

109

The startled Substitute gulped. "Uh—thank you . . . *Well*, according to Mr. Parkhill's instructions, we should devote ourselves to Open Questions. I am told you all keep notes, during the week, of all sorts of questions you intend to raise in class. If you will refer to them now, for *just* a few minutes. . . ."

Notebooks, tablets, scraps of paper, even a small box and two envelopes emerged from folders, purses, briefcases, and one basket. But Mr. Kaplan, to Mr. Jennings's discomfiture, consulted no record at all. Instead, he tilted his head to one side, closed both eyes, and whispered in a tone audible to one and all, "So ve stot Haupen Qvastions! . . . T'ree points. Foist, esk abot 'A room goink arond.' "

"I beg your pardon?" put in Mr. Jennings. "I didn't hear what you were saying."

Mr. Kaplan opened one optic organ. "I vasn't *say*ink, I vas *t'ink*ink."

"Oh, I'm sorry."

"Don't mantion it." Mr. Kaplan returned to vocal rumination. "Qvastion number two: Esk abot 'so-an-so.' "

Mr. Jennings's ears began to itch.

"Number t'ree, de *big* qvastion, esk—"

"Let us begin," called Mr. Jennings. "We shall recite in order, starting with—with the gentleman at the end of the back row, please." (That would leave Mr. Kaplan almost to the end.)

"De lest row *foist*?" cried Mr. Kaplan, a man betrayed.

"Shall we commence?" Mr. Jennings asked. "Mr.—?"

"Scymczak. Casimir Scymczak." The owner of this formidable name ran a hand across his crew-cut, sniffled, apologized, and inquired which was correct in refined company: to lift peas to one's mouth with a knife, spoon, or "fog."

"Well, now." Mr. Jennings merrily explained the difference between a fork and a fog. The explanation was so vivid that three pupils jeered at Mr. Scymczak.

Miss Rochelle Goldberg, who was next (she seemed to be chewing licorice), sought help with the spelling of "Tsintsinnati," where her brother lived. "I looked already five times in my dictionary, but there is no 'Tsintsinnati'!"

"Ah, *well,*" Mr. Jennings reassured her, "I'm afraid a dictionary will not help if you look in the wrong place. From the way you pronounced the name, I sus*pect* you looked under 'Ts'!"

"How did you *know?*" Miss Goldberg marveled.

"Goldboig should look under 's'!" advised Mr. Kaplan. " '*Sin*cin—' "

"No, no, Mr. Kaplan! 'S-i-n-' is not at *all* where the young lady should have looked. 'Cincinnati' begins with a 'c' . . ." He wrote the name on the board. "Next?"

A Mr. Karl Finsterwald declared that he was perplexed by when to use "beside" and when to use "besides."

"That's an *extremely* interesting question," said Mr. Jennings and analyzed the distinction, which stunned Mr. Blattberg.

Miss Gidwitz was in a quandary about the differences between "loan," "borrow," "lend," and "ask for cradit."

Mr. Jennings breezed through this thicket with such alacrity that the class rewarded him with "Ah"s and "Oh"s and one resounding "Aha!" of approbation (from Mr. Kaplan).

Mr. Oscar Trabish raised a rather puzzling query: "Why in a t'eater do they sell salami?"

*"Hanh?"* bawled Mr. Bloom.

*"Vhere?!"* demanded a homemaker.

"In t'eater, last vik-end!" yawned Mr. Trabish.

"Salami . . . ?" Mr. Jennings frowned. "In a *the*ater?"

The guffaw from Wolfgang Schmitt brought one and all erect. "I did zee zat show! It vass not salami; it vass 'Salomé'!"

Hilarity replaced mystification as the scholars grasped the magnitude of Mr. Trabish's howler: Miss Kipnis's giggle almost developed into hiccoughs, Mr. Perez's snorts swept two loose pages off the arm of his chair, and Mrs. Tomasic laughed so hard she had to readjust her dentures.

" 'Salomé!' " exclaimed Mr. Jennings.

"Salami is meat with garlic," indignant Tarnova intoned. "But Salomé donced with savon veils ond chopped off John Baptist's neck."

Mr. Trabish turned red and slumped into the refuge of slumber.

"Next . . . Miss—?"

"*Mrs.* Yanoff," puffed a lady all in black, who proceeded to inquire whether there wasn't something queer about the interrogative: "What time did you *came,* dollink?"

Mr. Jennings was ever so glad to deal with that. He demonstrated why "did came" was bad English, just as "did ate" or "did ran" would be. "You see, class, the 'did' serves to convert the next verb into the past tense!" He went even further, expatiating on how "do" and "did" function as invaluable auxiliaries to a verb ("Do you play tennis?" "Did he telephone the doctor?"), and how, in a different context, the tenses of "to do" provide unique emphasis ("She *did* strike the postman!" "You *do* believe in God!").

The class, which had seen Mr. Parkhill plow this very pasture a dozen times before, sent bright nods and gay murmurs to bolster Mr. Jennings's morale. "Notice how adding a 'do' or a 'did' to a *question* lends *much* greater force than if we had no 'do's or 'did's at our disposal!" A shudder shook the synod at the thought of such a calamity. "For example: *'Did* he kill the lion?' *'Do* you like turnips?' *'Does* the weather report predict showers?'!"

It pleased Mr. Jennings no end to notice how absorbed the class remained throughout the disquisition: how few coughed or wheezed or shuffled their feet; how many took

112

notes with those special smiles and private chuckles which testify to the pride of comprehension. "Suppose we try a few sentences—or questions—to illustrate these points! Anyone?"

"She *did* learn to tangle?" blurted Miss Ziev.

"Tang*o*," said Mr. Jennings. "Very good."

"*Did* he anlist in the French Foreign Luncheon?" called Mr. Pinsky.

"The French Foreign *Leg*ion!" Mr. Jennings, aghast, kept encouragement glued to his lips.

"Did he did his shempoo?" sallied Mrs. Moskowitz.

"No, no, Mrs. Moskowitz. The first 'did' makes the second 'did' incorrect. It's: 'Did he *do*—or take—his shampoo?'"

At this point, it occurred to Mr. Jennings that for the past fifteen minutes Mr. Kaplan had not uttered a word. He had raised not one question, answered not one invitation to supply an example. He had not even scoffed at a single volunteer's offering. Throughout the entire give-and-take that swirled around the interrogative or emphasizing aspects of "did," Hyman Kaplan remained as indifferent as a clam, except once, when he moved in his chair with undisguised impatience.

"Next."

The next gentleman was Gus Matsoukas, who asked whether "doodle" was an American type of noodle. This sent one yeoman into hysterics and another into a chant: "'Doodle-*noodle*? Noodle-*doodle*'?!"

"Well, sir," replied Mr. Jennings, ignoring the levity, "a 'doodle' is an aimless scribble, marks made when one is dawdling or day-dreaming. This sort of thing." On the board he chalked some scrawls and scratches, a cryptic fez, a bristling pretzel. "*These* are doodles."

"They look like chop suey," said Mr. Kaplan.

"Y-yes—and that is an interesting association, Mr. Kaplan, because although chop suey does not contain *noodles,*

113

so far as I know, chow mein contains a good many!"

"Is thees teacher a *cook?*" gasped Mrs. Rodriguez.

*"I* like chop suey!" announced Mr. Bloom.

"Stick on de point," coldly cut in Mr. Kaplan. "Matsoukas esked a qvastion an' he desoives a straight enser." He proceeded to ask it. "Matsoukas, do de Griks like soup?"

"Yos."

"So *you* like soup?"

"Yos."

"Mr. Kap—"

"You like different type *objeks* in your soup? Like rice? Peace? Domplings?"

"No."

"You like *noodles* in soup?"

"Mr. Kap—"

"No."

"Aha!" The inquisitor struck home. "So you *do* know vhat noodles are!"

"Mr. Kaplan!"

"So what's all crazy marks on blackboard??" Matsoukas demanded.

Mr. Kaplan waved airily. "Dose are boo-boos, not noodles. Mocks mitout minnink, ven your mindt is on *doodles."*

*"I* never make doodles!" the Athenian glowered.

"So anjoy noodles."

*"Gentle*men . . . class . . . !" Mr. Jennings had never dreamed that Open Questions could turn into guerrilla warfare. "Let our lesson proceed! Mrs . . . ?"

"Moskowitz. Sadie L. Moskowitz, Mrs." The corpulent dowager, who had never heretofore so much as hinted that an initial decorated her name, went into a repertoire of heaves and hoves before inquiring why "quiet" was sometimes spelled "q-u-i-t-e."

"Oh, those are *entirely* different words. Let me ex-

114

plain." Mr. Jennings did, but saw that Mrs. Moskowitz was bewildered by subtle discriminations. He hurried ahead. "Mr. . . . ?"

"Perez. Vincente Perez. Why we put 'e' on the end of 'tease'? Mr. Parkhill told us 's' to make the plural of *'tea.'* "

"But *'tease'* with an 's-e' is a word which has no relation whatsoever to 'tea' or 't-e-a-s' *without* an 'e.' " Mr. Jennings printed the crucial words on the board:

TEA

TEAS

TEASE

The exclamations would have done justice to the Aurora Borealis. So pleased was Mr. Jennings by such enthusiasm that before he fully realized what he was risking, he called upon Mr. Kaplan.

The man rose, his smile approaching ecstasy. No other student had risen, but there was something altogether fitting about Mr. Kaplan's elevation to address the forum. A rustle (of anticipation? of daggers being unsheathed? of armor buckling?) skimmed across the room. "Ladies an' gantleman an' Mr. Channink, who is doing soch a fine jop in dis emoigency—"

"Stop the *spitches!*" scowled Mr. Bloom.

"Enof!" growled Stanislaus Wilkomirski.

Mr. Kaplan heeded not the varlets. "Avery place I go, I am vatchink, listenink"—Mr. Kaplan narrowed his eyes to lend authenticity to "vatchink, listenink"—"for t'ings I should esk in cless durink Aupen Qvastions."

All this, Mr. Jennings discovered, was but overture.

"So de foist qvastion I esk is: Vat's de minnink fromm 'A room is goink arond'!"

" 'A *room* is going around?' " Mr. Jennings's face fell.

"A room is goink arond."

"Oy!" bassooned Mrs. Moskowitz. "Is dat a cuckoo!"

"*Som* qvastion!" chortled Sam Pinsky, slapping one cheek.

" 'A room is going around,' " re-echoed Mr. Jennings, in a delaying maneuver. "Well, the meaning of the words is simple, Mr. Kaplan. But I find the phrase—somewhat exceptional." Inspiration suddenly brightened his downy cheeks. "Of course, if one were dizzy, or faint, or *drunk*" (in Education 403, Professor Mullenbach had told his trainees never to mince words), "then one might say, 'I feel *as if* the room is going around.' "

Norman Bloom snickered. "Still an' all, a crazy quastion!"

"Mine dear Bloom," murmured Mr. Kaplan, "only crazy *pipple* esk crazy qvestions."

"*I'm* crazy?!" bridled Mr. Bloom. "*You* are—"

"Mr. Kaplan," Mr. Jennings quickly put in, "perhaps you could tell us where—I mean, in what circumstances you heard that phrase."

"Gledly. I hoid it fromm Mr. Skolsky (dat's de man livink opstairs) abot Mrs. Nalson (dat's de family livink *don*stairs). Mr. Skolsky told me, 'You know, I t'ink Mrs. Nelson vants a divorce!' So I esked, netcheral, 'How you know?' So Mr. Skolsky enswered: '*Avery*body's sayink dat. A room is goink arond.' "

" 'A *rumor's* going around!' " cried Mr. Jennings. "Oh, yes, of course! Why, that's an *excellent* phrase. Indeed, it uses an interesting word: 'rumor.' Let me explain that: 'rumor' refers to—"

Mr. Kaplan shot arrows of triumph at Norman Bloom, who was beating his fists on his thighs, and a superior leer at Mrs. Moskowitz, who seemed to have fallen into a manhole.

After Mr. Jennings had defined and illustrated "rumor," Mr. Kaplan beamed: "My! A *fine* axplination."

"Your next question?"

"I hoid an axpression, it sonds fonny. *Fonny*"—Mr.

Kaplan steered a warning glance toward Mr. Bloom—"not crazy . . . Vhat's de minnink frommm 'a so-an'-so'?"

Mr. Jennings stared at Mr. Kaplan miserably. " 'A so-and-so'?" he repeated cautiously. "That phrase is heard quite commonly, but it really is—well, it's a way of not using—profanity." Mr. Jennings paused, hoping some comment would come to his rescue. His hopes died in the silence. "Well, class . . . let me see. . . ." He wondered how he could explain profanity without using it. "Profanity means—cursing, swearing, using not nice language."

"Mr. *Kap*lan!" Miss Mitnick caught her breath in horror.

"Shame," hissed Olga Tarnova, "shame!"

Rochelle Goldberg fortified her modesty with a marzipan.

"Let me put it this way, class. Suppose Frank, say, wants to say something nasty—"

"Who's 'Frank'?" asked Mrs. Moskowitz.

Mr. Jennings wiped his palms. "*Any* Frank. I used the name only as an *example.*"

"Like 'X' an' 'Y,' Moskovitz," flashed Hyman Kaplan. "You forgot awreddy Mr. Pockheel's smot exemples 'X' an' 'Y'?!"

"*I* don't like 'X' and 'Y' *and* also Frank!"

"*You* don't like 'i' before 'e' except after 'c'!"

"Have a hot, Mr. Kaplin!" wailed Mrs. Shimmelfarb. "Give an *inch . . .*"

"Class . . . listen. Suppose someone—anyone"—Mr. Jennings lunged on—"wants to say something not nice about someone else—"

"He should sharup!" blurted Mr. Blattberg, touching his grandson's baby tooth as if to preserve its innocence.

"An' soppose he has to svear?!" cracked Mr. Kaplan.

"Mr. Kap—"

"Dat's de exect problem Mr. Channink is tryink to halp us ot mit! If a man vants to svear—"

"He should bite—his—tong!" retorted Miss Ziev.

117

*"Efter* he svears he ken bite his tong!" decreed the master.

"Give an *inch,* Mr. Kaplan," pleaded Mrs. Shimmelfarb. "Give an inch!"

Stern Kaplan rebuffed the apostle of compromise. "De essantial problem Titcher is tryink to axplain is how to svear by *not* svearing!"

"Precisely!" said Mr. Jennings. "That's a—forceful way of putting it." *Let* the faces of Mr. Kaplan's foes drop or darken: his ingenious elucidation had saved the day. "Someone who does not want to employ offensive or vulgar language *can* say, 'He's a so-and-so!' instead of—" Too late did young Jennings realize he had gone too far. "Instead of—"

The students leaned forward tensely.

"Instead of—" Mr. Jennings floundered.

"Low-life! Bum! Goot-fa-nottink!"

"Yes, Mr. Kaplan! Exactly!" Mr. Jennings almost choked with gratitude. "That's *precisely* how 'a so-and-so' is used!"

"Ah!"'s of admiration ululated down the ranks, but Mr. Bloom protested, "That still doesn't make Kaplen's quastion polite! *We have ladies in the room!"*

"Ve also have *lights,"* parried Mr. Kaplan, "so does dat minn ve should naver mantion sonshine?"

*"Mein Gott!"* railed Wolfgang Schmitt.

"Don't split a hair!" fumed Mr. Marcus.

"An *inch,"* begged Bessie Shimmelfarb, "for once, give—"

"Ladies! Gentlemen!" the Substitute shouted. "Do let us observe decorum!"

Decorum was alien to both the vocabulary and the ground rules of the embattled partisans. Miss Tarnova rushed to support Mr. Bloom's *politesse* with poisoned glares at Mr. Kaplan. Mr. Scymczak rallied to the Kaplan

118

banner with a counterthrust: "In class should be frenk and honest on all times!" Mrs. Rodriguez blared, "No dirt in clean houses!" To which stout Pinsky, his voice breaking into a falsetto, retorted, "If Keplen didn't ask, *how would you know it's doity?!*"

"Let Kaplon siddon!" shouted Karl Finsterwald.

"Kaplin, hooray!" rejoined Miss Ziev.

Miss Goldberg must have consumed two Tootsie Rolls during the melee, and Miss Mitnick was wringing her hands in futile offers of propitiation. (Mr. Nathan P. Nathan was not there to cheer her with laughter. He was, at that very moment, dribbling a basketball around "Pepi" Martino of the Canarsie Buckets.)

"Please! *Class!* Can we not respect one another's—" Mr. Jennings might just as well have been home with a cold, too.

"Keplen shouldn't bring street talk into class!" blazed Mrs. Tomasic.

"Shame, shame, Koplon!"

"Aha!" Mr. Kaplan's defiance resounded. "Tarnova, in education is no 'shame-shame' qvastions! Only ashamt *brains* make ashamt minninks!"

"Zat iss not zufficient excussess!" howled Wolfgang Schmitt.

"I hear bomble-bees," observed Mr. Kaplan.

"We are here to learn *nice* English!" protested "Cookie" Kipnis.

"Ve are here to loin averyt'ing!" rang out redoubtable Kaplan.

"Ooooy!"

And just when new attacks on Mr. Kaplan's indelicacy collided with fresh defenses of his purity of purpose, the cause of all the pandemonium raised an imperious hand. "I apolochize. It's all mine fault. I vas wronk!"

Tiberius himself could have received no swifter submission. Mr. Kaplan apologizing? Hyman Kaplan confessing he had erred? Down sank the contesting banners. Stilled were the combatants' voices. Passion oozed into murmurs.

"Yas, I made a beeg mistake!" Mr. Kaplan admitted. "De type 'so-an'-so' I hoid vas not de type 'so-an'-so' ve should make so many oguments abot."

"Watch for a trick," warned Mr. Vinograd.

"I dun't believe mine iss!" said Mrs. Yanoff, who had uncommonly large ears.

"It's no trick," sighed Mr. Kaplan. "It's a plain misondistendink. Listen. Here is vhat heppened. Lest vik, I mat Banny Kovarsky. A frand. Not a *close* frand, like fromm de old contry; still, a nice man. . . . Vell, Banny looked tarrible. His chiks pale. His ice sed, doll, mitout a spockle. His axpression vas like a man pulled ot of vater vhere—God fahbid—he could dron."

So bewildered was Mr. Jennings by the succession of solecisms, and so hypnotized by the unfolding tale, that he forgot all about his duty and corrected not one excruciating pronunciation.

"So I sad, 'Kovarsky, you look like you vaiting for an operation!' So Kovarsky pulled don his mot, silent. 'How you *fill?*' I esked. He sight, 'I vas seek. Not *dyink*. Seek.' So I continue, 'Bot now you fine?' He vent, 'Mnyeh.' So I looked on him mit full sympaty." Mr. Kaplan illustrated his sympathy by spreading wide his arms. " 'Banny, tell me de troot!' " his voice rang out. " 'How you fill *now?*' An' how did Kovarsky enswer? Like dis: 'Not jompink, but not in a coffin.' Dat Kovarsky! He is de type if you esk 'Vat time it is?' saz 'Maybe four o'clock, maybe fife.' In vun brat, Kovarsky can say 'Yas,' 'No,' 'Maybe' an' 'Vhy esk?'!"

"*Enof* awreddy!" boomed Norman Bloom.

"Make the *end!*" groaned Mr. Matsoukas.

"Tolstoy wos foster with *War and Peace!*" sneered Miss Tarnova.

Mr. Jennings roused himself. "Do—come to the point."

Mr. Kaplan dropped both hands wide to appease the multitude. "So efter all dis hammink and hawkink fromm dat *shlemiel* Kovarsky, I dimanded, rill lod: 'Stop bitink arond bushes! Do you fill *normal?* Do you fill *rotten?* Enswer!' . . . So how did he answer? He sad, 'I fill so-and-so'!"

"You mean 'so-*so*'!" cried Mr. Jennings. "Not 'so-*and*-so.' Of course! 'So-so!' That means not well, but not ill; not happy, but not gloomy. Just—it's an *ex*cellent colloquial expression—'so-so'!"

"Aaah," beamed Mr. Kaplan.

"Psssh!" psshed Mr. Pinsky, slapping both cheeks.

Mr. Bloom mopped his forehead, babbling.

The bell knelled in the corridor. At once the shoal of students surfaced, chattering and gossiping, wrestling into raincoats, snatching galoshes, fluttering umbrellas. It was pouring outside.

Mr. Jennings stood quite still, thinking. He wondered if he would ever forget that astounding evening. How could he report it, in all its flavor and tumult, to Professor Mullenbach? . . . He sat down and swiftly scrawled notes. He might have remained at Mr. Parkhill's desk for an hour had not a man with a mop and pail called from the doorway: "Mister, you expect to sleep here all night?"

"Oh. I'm sorry."

"Time to close."

"Yes, of course."

The man scratched his chin. "Young man, you feel all right?"

"What? . . . Certainly!" Mr. Jennings broke into a sweat; he had tottered on the very brink of replying, more accurately, "So-so."

121

# 11

## MR. K·A·P·L·A·N ' S
## UNSTAINED BANNER

It seemed only logical to Mr. Parkhill that, having introduced his students to the pitfalls of the Personal Letter, he should initiate them into Business Communications. Indeed, business letters could prove even more useful to the beginners' brigade: they might want to apply for a job or complain about a bill—or things of that sort.

For some time now, Mr. Parkhill had held off tackling Business Letters; but when he studied his outline for the remaining weeks of the semester, he realized that the schedule was becoming exceedingly crowded. It was foolhardy to delay any longer. *"Tempus* does *fugit* swifter than one realizes!"* was what he concluded.

"The general form of a business letter follows that of the personal letter," said Mr. Parkhill briskly. "It, too, requires your home address, the date, a salutation, a final greeting—or, as some call it, 'the complimentary close.'" He went on to explain that the business letter was, of course, more official in mood; that the address of the person or company to whom one wrote had to be placed on the left-hand side; that both salutation and final greeting were formalized—the former being "Dear Sir," "Dear Sirs," or "Gentlemen," and the latter "Yours truly," "Yours very truly," or "Very truly yours." Mr.

Parkhill described Business Letters with considerable patience.

All had gone well, very well, so well that Mr. Parkhill held high hopes for the homework he had assigned: "A Short Business Letter." Now six students were transcribing their chore on the blackboard. Miss Valuskas, commendably ambitious, was applying for a position as secretary to the president of the zoo. (Miss Valuskas was admired by all her colleagues for her familiarity with animals.) Mr. Feigenbaum was ordering "1 dozen shirts size 15" from the emporium he called "Orbox." Mr. Norman Bloom, the soul of efficiency, was inscribing a note to "S. Levin, Jobbers," curtly reminding them that they owed him $217.75 for merchandise "lust in transit." (The debt was fictitious, of course: Mr. Bloom made pockets for Never-Leak Raincoats.) Miss Fanny Gidwitz was chalking a polite order to "Alexanger" for a sport coat and "pair gloffs" she wished delivered "C.O.T."

At the corner of the room, next to the door, Hyman Kaplan was stationed. Sheer incandescence adorned Mr. Kaplan's smile this evening, and something of Rembrandt distinguished his posture. The blackboard might have been a canvas, for Mr. Kaplan kept his left hand behind his back as he stepped back and forth, eyes narrowed, in periodic appraisal of the wonders his right hand transferred to the slate from the notebook propped on the blackboard's ledge. Both the smile and the stance made Mr. Parkhill uneasy. No sooner had Mr. Kaplan completed his business letter than Mr. Parkhill's eyes raced straight through it:

459 E. 3. Street
New York
Janu. 8

Joseph Mandelbaum
A-1 Furniture Comp.
741 Broadway
New York
NY
USA

Dear Sir Mandelbaum—

Sarah and me want to buy a refrigidator. Always she tells me "Hymie, our eyes-box is terrible. Old. Leeking." This is true.

Because you are in furniture, I am writing about. How much will cost a refrigidator? It must not have a short circus. The 1 we have, brakes a fuze each time I close the door. I told Sarah "Do not full around with laktricity!"

So please xamine your stock. If your eye falls on a bargain pick it up.

Very Truly Wating,
H*Y*M*A*N  K*A*P*L*A*N
(Address on Top)

P.S.  Best regards from Sarah:

With all kinds fond fillings,
H*Y*M*I*E

When the last member of the platoon left the board, Mr. Parkhill said, "I think we had better take Mr. Kaplan's letter first." (Customarily, recitations started at the *left* side, but Mr. Parkhill determined to face the worst first.)

"Me *foist?*" Mr. Kaplan was transmogrified.

"Yes."

"My!" By the time Mr. Kaplan reached the board his smile was supernal. "Ladies an' gantleman, in dis lasson I falt—"

"Mr. Kaplan," Mr. Parkhill broke in, "just read your letter. There is no need for an—er—introduction."

Only Mr. Kaplan's pride in being first sustained him in so crushing a rebuff. "Podden me." He turned to the letter. " 'Dear Sir Mendelbum . . .' "

"Holy mackinel!" exploded Norman Bloom. " 'Dear *Sir* Mandelbum'?"

"Maybe he iss in the Houze of Lords," snorted Wolfgang Schmitt.

"Kaplan, look noble!" laughed Mr. Wilkomirski.

Mr. Parkhill tapped his pointer rapidly. "Let us hold all comments until Mr. Kaplan has finished."

Mr. Kaplan's squint at Mr. Bloom would have cowed an Apache. " 'Dear Sir Mendelbum,' " he repeated. " 'Sarah vants to buy a refrigidator.' "

*"Hanh?"* came through Mr. Finsterwald's adenoids.

"He means a refrigi *mak*er!" called Miss Pomeranz.

"Eet weel break *don* as soon he opens the door!" predicted Mrs. Rodriguez.

" 'Always she tells me "Hymie . . ." ' " Deaf to the bleatings and protestations of the *hoi polloi,* Mr. Kaplan read on in the cadence of dignity. He uttered the final words with regret. " 'Wit all kinds fon fillings, Hymie.' " His features simulated modesty. "Dat's de and."

"Thonk God," crooned Olga Tarnova.

"Good-*bye* English!" croaked Mr. Blattberg. (Mr. Blattberg had begun to foretell the death of English whenever Mr. Kaplan began *or* finished a recitation.)

"Class," said Mr. Parkhill, "everyone will have a chance to comment. But let me begin by asking Mr. Kaplan—do you think that that is—er—strictly a *bus*iness letter?"

"It's *abot* business . . ."

"But certain phrases, quite *personal* passages, the final greeting—" Mr. Parkhill paused. "I shall ask the class to comment. Who would like to start off?"

Everyone wanted to start off: Mr. Bloom was rolling his

eyes as wildly as his hand was punching the air; Miss Valuskas had *both* hands raised; Mr. Matsoukas was muttering cryptic emendations; Mrs. Tomasic's ruler was whirling around like a windmill.

Mr. Parkhill rejected the bloodthirsty; experience warned him to steer clear of vehemence at the outset. He glanced around . . . and happily beheld the small, still palm of Rose Mitnick, at whom Nathan P. Nathan was winking incentive.

"Miss Mitnick!"

"In my opinion," the sedate maid blushed, "Mr. Kaplan's letter is not a business one. Because in a business letter, you don't tell your wife's first name. And you don't send 'best regards.' And 'all kinds fond feelings' is only for *personal* letters!"

"Maybe dis is a *poissonal* business ladder?" crafty Kaplan murmured.

Miss Mitnick, startled for but an instant, demolished the sophistry. "No, Mr. Kaplan. I think it is *wrong* to give family facts in a business letter! It's not the business of a company to know what a wife is saying to a husband, or a husband to a wife!"

"Very good, Miss—"

"Mitnick," warned Mr. Kaplan, "you forgat to *who* I wrote—"

"That has nothing to do with it," Mr. Parkhill cut in. "Miss Mitnick is entirely right. One doesn't discuss personal details or family affairs in a business communication—which is, after all, to an organization, to strangers."

"Mendelbum," sighed Mr. Kaplan, "is mine oncle."

Twenty-eight throats uttered twenty-eight outcries, which roused Mr. Trabish out of somnolence and into bewilderment. Mr. Pinsky crowed "Psssh! Psssh!" over the cunning of his chieftain. Poor Miss Mitnick, the color of wax, bleated. Mr. Nathan, forfeiting affection for the moment, erupted loud laughter.

*"Mr.* Kaplan!" exclaimed Mr. Parkhill. *"If* that letter *is* really addressed to your—er—uncle, then it should not be called a business communication in the first place!"

"Vell, I edmit dat fect boddered me, too," conceded Mr. Kaplan. "If I am buyink a refrigida—"

" 'Refrigerator'!"

"—a refrigerator, buyink *is* business. Dat's vhy in de foist pot fromm de ladder—"

" *'Let*ter,' Mr. Kap—"

"—I wrote cold, formal, stock-op." Mr. Kaplan elevated his nose to illustrate "stock-op." "But den, I falt it is time to show som family *fillink.* An oncle is an oncle! So I put don 'bast rigotts from Sarah—' "

"And is 'best regards' right for a business letter?" stammered Miss Mitnick.

"It's *spalled* right," parried Mr. Kaplan.

"Koplon!" howled Olga Tarnova.

"A *trick!*" fumed Norman Bloom.

"Give an inch, Mr. Kaplan, give an *inch,*" wailed Mrs. Shimmelfarb.

"He won't give an *ounce,*" grinned Mr. Pinsky.

"He avoids the ezential izue!" seethed Wolfgang Schmitt.

"His 'Yes' is 'Maybe' and his 'No' is 'Who cares?' " stormed Mr. Blattberg.

Mr. Parkhill rapped the pointer on his desk with certitude. "Mr. Kaplan . . . the objections are well taken. As Miss Mitnick put it, quite correctly, you cannot *combine* two forms. Either you write a business letter or you write a personal letter!"

Mr. Blattberg chortled, Mrs. Tomasic snickered, Miss Caravello applauded with rapture.

Mr. Parkhill warned Mr. Kaplan that in the future he write personal letters only to friends or relatives, and business communications to total strangers. "Now let's turn to the other mistakes—of which, I may say, there are many."

"The mistakes by Kaplen are like customers at a fire sale!" cried Norman Bloom. " 'Sarah and me' should be 'Sarah and I.' And 'eyes-box'?! Phooey! 'I-c-e' means 'ice'; 'e-y-e-s' means *'eyes.'* One is for seeing, the other for freezing!"

No sally of Oscar Wilde's ever elicited greater mirth.

Miss Ziev crowed that "leaking" was spelled wrong. Karl Finsterwald added, "And so is 'examine.' " Miss Valuskas remarked caustically that there should be no capitals after "very" in "Very truly" and cast doubts on the legitimacy of "Very Truly Waiting," adding: "Also a mistake in its spelling, for is missing 'i.' " Mr. Marcus was all irony as he intimated that Mr. Mandelbaum was probably wise enough to read Mr. Kaplan's address without being told to look for it in "Address on Top." Even stolid Mrs. Yanoff leaped into the autopsy. "I know one thing," she said, smoothing her black dress. "A circus is with alephants, clons, and flying tepees. So you can't put a circus in a refrigerator, not even a *'short* circus'!"

"You don't know abot laktric," charged Mr. Kaplan.

"Elactric, gez, even cendles!" Mrs. Moskowitz dived into the lists. "A soicus won't fit insite an ice-box!"

"Maybe de kind *you* minn," began Mr. Kaplan, "bot—"

Mr. Parkhill rapped the desk firmly. "You don't mean 'short *circus,'* Mr. Kaplan. You mean 'short *circuit.'* " He wrote both words on the board. " 'C-i-r-c-u-i-t,' Mr. Kaplan, not 'c-i-r-c-u-s.' They are entirely different words!"

"De resamblance is remockable," observed Hyman Kaplan.

Mr. Nathan doubled over.

"I see another mistake!" called Miss Mitnick. "In Mr. Kaplan's letter is the line: 'If your eye falls on a bargain, pick it up.' " Flushed, Miss Mitnick repeated: "If your *eye* falls on a bargain pick *it* up!"

Hilarity convulsed the arena: laughs, hoots, taunts; jeers

of derision danced among caterwauls of scorn.

Mr. Parkhill was puzzled by Mr. Kaplan's airy acceptance of such rank ridicule; then he noticed that the smile Mr. Kaplan smiled was as close to revealing an ambush as any smile can be.

"An' vhat's wronk, Mitnick?" asked Mr. Kaplan. "Vhat's de exect mistake?"

"You don't *zee?*" cracked Mr. Schmitt.

"N-no . . ." grinned Mr. Kaplan.

Mr. Bloom, who should have been warned by Mr. Kaplan's blithe demeanor, now crowed like a rooster. " 'If your *eye* falls on a bargain please pick *it* up?' 'It?' The *eye?!!*"

Then Mr. Kaplan struck. "Mine oncle," he said, "has a gless eye."

Mr. Bloom's jaw fell apart. Mrs. Moskowitz collapsed. Miss Mitnick whinnied. Mr. Nathan was choking in elation. Olga Tarnova gasped Russian maledictions. Mr. Pinsky cried, "Ginius! Keplen is an ebsolute ginius!"

And Mr. Kaplan's smile was as serene as a child's, deep in a dream of glory. He had routed an ignoble legion. He had demolished his petty foes. Once again he had snatched victory from the very teeth of defeat. His honor, unstained, waved above him like a pure white banner.

# 12

## THE DEATH OF
## JULIUS CAESAR

It was Miss Higby's idea. (At least, Mr. Parkhill reflected, it had all started that way.) One night in the faculty lounge, Miss Higby remarked how unfortunate it was that students came to her class wholly unaware of the *finer* side of English, of its beauty and grandeur, of (as she put it) "the glorious heritage of our literature." "There is no reason on earth," Miss Higby had blurted, "why the beginners' grade might not be introduced to a *taste*, at least, of Longfellow or Tennyson or—even Shakespeare!"

Mr. Parkhill could not deny that there was much to be said for Miss Higby's point of view. His pupils *were* adults, after all; they had come to our shores from lands renowned for poets and scholars and men of letters; and many a fledgling in English referred, on occasion, to some classic of European literature. Mr. Matsoukas, for all his cryptic grunts and saturnine moods, sometimes tossed off names from the *Iliad* with considerable fervor. Miss Tarnova (who could wring lurid overtones from a telephone number) rarely let slip by a chance to extol Tolstoy or Gogol or Lermontov. Wolfgang Schmitt, who had gone halfway through a *gymnasium* in Ulm, once delivered an impassioned testimonial to great Thomas Mann. ("Who said he vas a voman?" Mr. Kaplan had scoffed.) And any number of others in the beginners' grade had seen one or another production, in their native tongue, of *Hamlet* or *The Cherry Orchard, Cyrano de Bergerac* or *A Doll's House* (whose author had unfortunately been identified by Nathan P. Nathan as "Henry Gibson").

Apart from Miss Higby's effusive recommendation, Mr. Parkhill realized that his students had been studying English for some time now; they had added *hundreds* of words and phrases to their vocabularies; they had reached a level of familiarity with their new tongue which few teachers would have thought possible when the term began.

"Poetry will alert your class to more precise enunciation," Miss Higby had gone on to say, "and may even attune their ears to the subtleties of English inflection!" (Miss Higby, whose master's thesis was on Coventry Patmore, *loved* poetry.)

Mr. Parkhill had remarked, "I just wonder whether my beginners may not feel a bit beyond their depth—"

"Nonsense!" Miss Higby promptly retorted. "As Plaut and Samish dis*tinct*ly state in their final chapter. . . ."

That was the crowning argument. No one teaching English to foreigners could fault a fiat from the magisterial opus of Plaut and Samish.

So it was that when he faced the class the next Tuesday night, a beautiful night, soft and smelling of spring, Mr. Parkhill produced his portable Shakespeare. The love Miss Higby felt for poetry in general was nothing compared to the love Mr. Parkhill bore for Shakespeare in particular. (How many years was it since he had played Polonius at Amherst?)

"Tonight, class," Mr. Parkhill smiled, "I am going to try a little—experiment."

Thirty heads swung upward. Sixty eyes turned guarded. The beginners' grade had learned to regard Mr. Parkhill's innovations with foreboding.

"We shall take a little excursion into poetry—great poetry—from the greatest master English has ever known. . . ." Mr. Parkhill delivered a little sermon on the special beauty of poetry, its charm and precision and economy, its revelation of the loftiest thoughts and emotions of mankind. "I think this will be a welcome relief, to all of us, from our—er—run-of-the-mill exercises!" The approving nods and murmurs heartened Mr. Parkhill no end. "So . . . I shall write a famous passage on the board. I shall read it for you. Then, as our Recitation and Speech exercise, you will give short addresses, using the passage as the—springboard, as it were, for your own interpretation: your own thoughts and ideas and reactions."

He could not remember the last time an announcement had so roused the rows before him.

"Bravo!" sang Carmen Caravello.

"How my mohther did lof Heinrich Heine," sighed Mr. Finsterwald.

Miss Mitnick blushed, mingling pride and wonder. Mr. Bloom clucked—but rather cagily. Mrs. Rodriguez wrinkled her nose: *her* last foray into loftiness was a speech praising Brooklyn Bridge. And Hyman Kaplan, the smile on his face more salubrious than ever, showered Mr. Parkhill with expressions of admiration, whispering: "Poyetry. Now is poyetry! My! Must be som progriss ve makink!"

"The passage," said Mr. Parkhill, "is from Shakespeare."

A bolt of lightning could not have electrified the room more than did the magic of that name.

"*Shakes*peare?!" echoed Mr. Perez. "Eee-ai-ee!"

"The greatest poet from English?" gasped Miss Ziev.

"Imachine!" murmured Mr. Kaplan. "Villiam Jakesbeer!"

" '*Shakes*peare,' Mr. Kaplan, not '*Jakesb*eer'!"

Mr. Parkhill took a fresh stick of chalk to write the passage on the board in large, crystal-clear letters:

> Tomorrow, and tomorrow, and tomorrow
> Creeps in this petty pace from day to day,
> To the last syllable of recorded time;
> And all our yesterdays have lighted fools
> The way to dusty death.

"Be*aur*iful!" glowed Mr. Kaplan.

>                     Out, out, brief candle!
> Life's but a walking shadow, a poor player
> That struts and frets his hour upon the stage,
> And then is heard no more; it is a tale
> Told by an idiot—

"True; sod, but true," moaned Olga Tarnova.

>                     —full of sound and fury,
> Signifying nothing.

The hush of consecration muffled that mundane chamber. Open mouths and suspended breaths, gulps of awe and gapes of reverence edified the eyes that drank in the deathless phrases of the immortal bard. Even Nathan P. Nathan sat solemn.

Mr. Parkhill cleared his throat. "I shall read the passage aloud. Please listen carefully; let Shakespeare's words—I know some are difficult—sink into your minds . . . 'Tomorrow, and tomorrow and tomorrow . . .' " Mr. Parkhill read very well; and this night he endowed each word with an eloquence even Miss Higby would have admired. " 'Out, out, brief candle!' " Miss Mitnick's face was bathed in wonderment. " 'Life's but a walking shadow . . .' " The brow of Gus Matsoukas furrowed. " 'It is a tale told by an idiot . . .' " Mr. Kaplan's cheeks were incandescent. " '. . . full of sound and fury . . .' " Mr. Trabish's eyes were shut. (Mr.

Parkhill could not tell whether Mr. Trabish had surrendered to the spell of Shakespeare or the arms of Morpheus.) "'. . . signifying nothing!'" Miss Goldberg fumbled for a jellybean.

"I—shall read the passage once more." Mr. Parkhill's voice was so loud and clear that it roused Mr. Trabish from his coma. "'Tomorrow, and tomorrow, and tomorrow . . .'"

After Mr. Parkhill completed that incomparable passage, he surveyed his congregation gravely. "I am sure there are words, here and there, which some of you may find—uh—difficult. Before I call upon you to recite, please feel free to ask—"

Freedom of inquiry erupted within the instant. Mrs. Tomasic asked if "petty" was the diminutive of "pet." (Mr. Parkhill could scarcely blame her for asking if it could be used for her neighbor's "small white rabbi.") Wolfgang Schmitt asked why "frets" lacked a capital "f." (The meticulous butcher thought "frets" was the Americanized form of "Fritz.") Mrs. Shimmelfarb wondered whether "creeps" was a variation of "creaks." Miss Gidwitz, who was exceedingly clothes-conscious, asked if "fury" was the "old-fashion" way of spelling "furry" (her new coat was a beautiful "tweet" with "a furry collar").

Each of these queries Mr. Parkhill explained with patience. "'Petty' means trivial, mean, or—not worthy, as in 'Jealous people tend to be petty.' . . . 'Frets,' Mr. Schmitt, means to be impatient, showing discontent, as in 'She frets because her train is late!' . . . 'Creeps,' Mrs. Shimmelfarb, means to move slowly, *very* slowly; for instance, 'A turtle *creeps* through the grass.' . . . And 'fury,' Miss Gidwitz, denotes a powerful emotion, not an animal's—er—hide. . . . Anyone else?"

Up stabbed the finger of Casimir Scymczak. "Why," he mumbled, "is no 'l' in word 'pace'? Wrong spalled?!" Mr. Parkhill saw in a flash that Mr. Scymczak was confusing

134

motion with location. "The spelling is entirely correct: you see, *'pace'* is in no way related to *'place.'* " Mr. Parkhill found, to his surprise, that he was beginning to perspire. " 'Pace' means the rate or speed of movement, as 'The soldiers marched at a brisk pace,' or 'The cars moved in slow, respectful pace to the cemetery.' "

This saddened Mr. Scymczak.

"Are we ready now, class?"

"No!" came from sultry Miss Tarnova. "Did Shakespeare steal that whole idea from Dostoevsky?!"

Before Mr. Parkhill could nip this delusion in the bud, Mr. Kaplan wheeled around. "Are you *crazy?* You talkink about *Jakes*beer!"

*"Shakes*peare, Mr.—"

"I'm sick an' tiret hearing soch chipp remocks. Lat's begin recitink!"

Mr. Parkhill wiped his palms. (He felt rather grateful to Mr. Kaplan.) "Very well, class . . . Miss Caravello."

Miss Caravello lunged to the podium. "Da poem isa gooda!" she proclaimed. "Itsa have beautiful wordsa, *bella*, lak great musica anda deepa, deepa philosophy. Shakespeare isa lak Alighieri Dante, da greatest Italiano—"

"Vhat?!" bristled Mr. Kaplan. "Shakesbeer you compare mit Dante? *Shakesbeer?!* Ha!"

"Mr. Kaplan, Miss Caravello is merely expressing her opinion."

"Dat's not an opinion, it's a crime! How ken she compare a ginius like Shakesbeer mit a dantist like Dante?!"

"Dante wasa no dentist!" fumed Miss Caravello. "He—"

"He didn't iven stody *teet?"* purred Mr. Kaplan.

Miss Caravello blazed an execration from her homeland and shot back to her seat, gibbering calumnies worthy of Juvenal. Mrs. Shimmelfarb soothed her with sympathy. Miss Goldberg offered her a sourball.

Mr. Parkhill felt dizzy.

"Corrections, anyone?"

Aside from Mr. Trabish's sleepy remark anent Miss Caravello's tendency to add the vowel "a" to any word in sight, and a gritty observation from Mr. Perez that *"bella"* was a foreign word "and we supposed dzhust to talk English!" criticism expired.

The next speaker, Mrs. Yanoff, began, "This pome is full high meanings." Her eyes, however, were fixed on the floor. "Is hard for a person who is not so good in English to catch all. But I like."

" 'Like'?!" flared Mr. Kaplan. "Batter *love,* Yanoff! Mit Shakesbeer must be *love!"*

*"Mr.* Kaplan . . ."

Mrs. Yanoff staggered through several skittish comments and stumbled back to safety.

Next came Norman Bloom. Mr. Kaplan groaned. Mr. Bloom was as brisk, bald, and emphatic as ever. Only his peroration was unexpected: "But Shakespeare's *ideas* are too passimistical. I am an optimist. Life should be with hope and happy! . . . So, remember—this is only a poem, by a man full of gloomy! I say, 'Mr. Shakespeare, why don't you look for a silver lining on the sonny side of each street?' "

"Bloooom!" bawled anguished Kaplan. "You forgat how *honist* is Shakesbeer! He is a passimist because *life* is a passimist also!"

"Not *my* life!" sneered Mr. Bloom.

"You not dad yat," observed Mr. Kaplan, not without regret.

Nathan P. Nathan caterwauled.

"Gentlemen!" Mr. Parkhill was growing quite alarmed. It was clear that Mr. Kaplan had so identified himself with Shakespeare that he would not tolerate the slightest disparagement of his alter ego. How harness so irate a champion? How dampen such flames of grandeur? Perhaps the

136

best course (Mr. Parkhill stifled many misgivings) was to call on Mr. Kaplan at once.

After pointing out several flaws in Mr. Bloom's syntax, and the thoroughly improper use of "gloomy" as a noun, Mr. Parkhill said, "Mr. Kaplan, you—er—seem to be bubbling with so many ideas, perhaps you—would prefer to recite?"

The smile that spread across Mr. Kaplan's countenance rivaled a rainbow. *"Me* next?" The innocent blink of surprise, the fluttering lashes of unworthiness—rarely was modesty so fraudulent.

"Yes."

"Now comes the circus!" announced laughing Nathan. "Rose, get ready all your penecils and all your paper!"

"Go, Keplen!" grinned Mr. Pinsky.

"Trobble, trobble," moaned Olga Tarnova.

"For God's sek, talk *briff!*" growled Mr. Blattberg.

"Give him a *chence!*" snapped "Cookie" Kipnis.

"Oyyy," forecast Mrs. Moskowitz.

Mr. Kaplan rose with dignity, slowly, affecting the manner of one lost in unutterable profundities. In stately stride he mounted the platform. He clutched his lapels à la Daniel Webster. Never had the plump figure appeared so lordly, or displayed such consciousness of a rendezvous with history. He surveyed the ranks before him, thoughtful, silent, deliberating how to clothe majesty in words fit for commoners.

"Omi*god!*" blared Mr. Blattberg.

"So *talk!*" glowered Mr. Matsoukas.

"You are waiting for *bugles?*" taunted Miss Valuskas.

Mr. Kaplan ignored the carping crowd. "Fallow lovers of fine literature. Edmirers of immortable poyetry."

" 'Immor*tal,* ' " Mr. Parkhill put in. (He would not have been surprised if Mr. Kaplan had launched into "Friends, Romans, countrymen . . .") "And it's *'po-*etry,' not *'poy-*

etry.' If you will try to speak more slowly, Mr. Kaplan, I'm sure you will make fewer mistakes."

Mr. Kaplan inclined his head graciously. "So I'll begin over . . . Ladies an' gantlemen . . . Ve hoid fine spitches by odder mambers of de cless abot dese vunderful voi—*words* from Shakesbeer. Vell, are you sarisfite?"

" 'Satisfie*d*'!"

"Not me. I am ebsolutely not sa*t*isfite. Because to me dose movvelous *w*ords on de blackboard are not *w*ords! Dey are jools! Poils! Diamonds!"

"Psssh!" crowed Mr. Pinsky.

"T'ink abot it, cless. T'ink *bilow* an' *arond* dose ectual phrases Shakesbeer put in de mot of—of who? Dat's de important point! *Who is talkink?* A man mit a tarrible problem lookink him in de face. Try to remember how dat man, Julius Scissor, himsalf falt—"

"*Mr.* Kaplan! It was *not* Julius—"

The eulogist heard him not. "—on dat historical night! Because in dose movvelous *w*ords on dis simple bleckboard"—he flung out his right arm, as if from under a toga, pointing to the fateful passage—"Julius Scissor is sayink—"

"Mr. *Kap*lan! That passage is from *Macbeth!*"

Hyman Kaplan stopped in his tracks. He stared at his master as if at his executioner. "*Not* from *Julius Scissor?!*"

"No, no!"

Mr. Kaplan gulped. "I vas sure—"

"The passage is from *Macbeth,* Mr. Kaplan. And it's not Julius 'S*cis*sor'—but Julius C*aes*ar!"

Woe drowned the once lofty countenance. "Excuse me. But isn't a 'seezor' vhat you cottink somt'ink op mit?"

"That," said Mr. Parkhill, "is '*sci*ssor.' You have used 'Caesar' for 'scissor' and 'scissor' for 'Caesar'!"

"My!" Mr. Kaplan was marveling at his virtuosity.

Mr. Parkhill stood shaken. He blamed himself for not

having announced at the very beginning that the passage was from *Macbeth*. "Mr. Kaplan, may I ask what on earth made you think that the passage is from *Julius Caesar?*"

"Because I see it all before mine two ice! De whole scinn —just like a movie. Ve are in Julius's tant. It's de night bafore dey making him Kink fromm Rome. So he is axcited, netcheral, an' he ken't slip—"

" 'Sleep.' "

"—so he's layink in his bad, t'inking: 'Tomorrow an' tomorrow an' tomorrow. How slow dey movink. Dey practically cripp. Soch a pity de pace!' "

Before Mr. Parkhill could protest that "petty pace" did not mean "Soch a pity de pace!" Mr. Kaplan, batteries recharged, had swept ahead: "An' he t'inks: 'Oh, how de time goes slow, fromm day to day, like leetle tsyllables on phonograph racords of time.' "

"Mr. Kap—"

" 'An' vhat abot yastidday?' esks Julius Scissor. Ha!" Mr. Kaplan's eyes blazed. " 'All our yastiddays are only a light for fools to die in de dost!' "

" 'Dusty death' does not mean—" But no dam could block that mighty flood.

"An' Julius Scissor is so tiret, an' vants to slip, so he hollers, mit fillink, 'Go ot, go ot, short candle!' "

Mr. Parkhill sank into a chair.

"So de candle goes ot." Mr. Kaplan's voice dropped to a whisper. "Still, pracious slip von't come to Julius. Now is bodderink him de whole idea fromm Life. 'Vhat is Life altogadder?' t'inks Julius Scissor. An' he gives his own soch an enswer!—de pot of dat pessitch I like bast!"

" '*Pas*sage,' " groped Mr. Parkhill.

" 'Life is like a bum actor, strottink an' hollerink arond de stage for vun hour bafore he's kicked ot! *Life?* Ha! It's a pail full of idjots—' "

"No, *no!* A *'tale'* not a *'pail'*—"

" '—full of funny sonds an' phooey!' "

" 'Sound and fury!' " cried the frantic tutor.

" 'Life is monkey business! It don't minn a t'ing! It single-flies nottink!' . . . Den Julius closes his ice fest"—Mr. Kaplan demonstrated Caesar's exact ocular process by closing his own "ice"—"an' drops dad!"

Silence throbbed its threnody in that hall of learning. Even Miss Tarnova, Mr. Blattberg, flighty Miss Gidwitz sat magnetized by such eloquence. Nathan P. Nathan was holding Miss Mitnick's hand. Miss Goldberg sucked a mint.

Mr. Kaplan nodded philosophically. "Yas, Scissor, great Scissor, dropped dad, forever!" He left the hallowed podium. But just before he took his seat, Mr. Kaplan added this postscript: "Dat vas mine idea. But ufcawss it's all wronk, because Mr. Pockheel axplained how it's not abot Julius Scissor altogadder." A sigh. "It's abot an Irishman by de name MacBat!"

It seemed an age before Mr. Parkhill reached his desk, and another before he could bring himself to concentrate on Mr. Kaplan's memorial. For Mr. Parkhill found it hard to wrench his mind back to the cold world of grammar and syntax. Like his students, he was still trying to tear himself away from that historic tent outside Rome, where "Julius Scissor," cursed with insomnia, had pondered time and life, and philosophized himself to a strange and sudden death.

Mr. Parkhill felt distinctly annoyed with Miss Higby.

140

# 13

## VOCABULARY, VOCABULARY!

"Vocabulary!" Mr. Parkhill thought. "Above all, I must help them increase their vocabularies."

He was probably right. What the students in the beginners' grade most needed, what they could put to instant use, was a copious supply of words: English words, words for naming ordinary objects, asking simple questions, describing everyday experiences. If one weighted the respective merits of vocabulary and, say, spelling, as Mr. Parkhill had spent many an hour doing, one would be forced to decide in favor of devoting more time to the former than the latter. However basic spelling is (and to Mr. Parkhill nothing was more basic) it is nonetheless not so pressing *outside* a classroom to adults who do little actual writing in their daily work and life.

"After all," Mr. Parkhill had put it to Miss Higby, "one does not need to know how to *spell* English in order to use it!"

"Our students certainly prove that," Miss Higby had replied.

What about grammar? Mr. Parkhill had spent an entire weekend debating the comparative importance of vocabulary and grammar. What he concluded was that for newcomers, vocabulary must be given priority over grammar. His pupils needed words, phrases, idioms to which grammar could be *applied.* Of what use is grammar, after all, until one had the words to use that grammar on? Grammar without words was like—well, like a useless skeleton. And one needed the word "skeleton" before one could even say what a skeleton *is.*

"Words are the basic *bricks,*" he said to Miss Higby, "whereas grammar is the building."

Miss Higby gazed at him in admiration. "Have you just made that up, Mr. Parkhill?"

"I think so."

"But that's very *good!*" exclaimed Miss Higby. "Why, it's more graphic than anything in Plaut and Samish!" (That was just about as high praise as anyone could receive from Miss Higby.)

What about pronunciation? There certainly was a strong, strong case to be made for pronunciation. (Only last Tuesday, Mr. Hyman Kaplan had waxed lyrical about such favorite foods as "rose beef, cinema toast, and pie à-la-Moe.") Mr. Parkhill often toyed with the unhappy idea that correct English pronunciation might simply be beyond some of his fledglings' capacities.

Take the "th" sound. What could appear so simple? Yet Mr. Wolfgang Schmitt had spoken German for so many years before coming to the American Night Preparatory School for Adults that his tongue-and-teeth coordination were frozen into patterns which just could not pronounce the "th" except as "s." (In one recitation, it was impossible to know whether Mr. Schmitt was discussing "themes" or "seams.") Other students would never be able to pronounce the "th" except as "z." (It had unnerved Mr. Parkhill to hear Mr. Finsterwald describe a political rally in which "zree zousant zroats" had acclaimed the speaker.) Or take Mr. Kaplan. Mr. Parkhill sighed. (He had fallen into the habit of sighing whenever Mr. Kaplan invaded his ruminations.) Mr. Kaplan was a willing, diligent student.

142

Yet, despite Mr. Parkhill's persistent lecturings about the need to exercise care in pronouncing words, Mr. Kaplan had recently said of the Mayor of New York that he showed a fine set of teeth "vhenever he greens." Another time, so deceived could Mr. Kaplan's *hearing* be, when asked to use "heaven" in a sentence, he had replied: "In sommer, ve all heaven a fine time."

At that moment, Mr. Parkhill had spotted an important linkage between vocabulary *and* pronunciation: to teach one could produce the side-effect of *teaching the other, too!* Mr. Parkhill had scarcely been able to sleep, one night, so full was his mind with the methods he would employ to teach his flock vocabulary in such a way that they would see the crucial difference between, say, "these" and "seize"—or even between "box" and "bucks." (It was terribly confusing to have a student talk about money all the while Mr. Parkhill thought he was referring to deer.)

Vocabulary! The last shred of doubt vanished from Mr. Parkhill's mind. He could hardly wait for the evening to come.

". . . so tonight I shall call off a list of words, simple, *useful* words, words which you will find helpful in your daily life. I shall assign three words to each of you. Write three sentences in your notebook, using each word in a separate sentence . . . Miss Valuskas? Yes, you certainly may use your dictionary . . . When you are finished, go to the board and copy your sentences."

The class seemed quite pleased by vocabulary. Miss Mitnick's self-effacing pallor changed to one of pink eagerness. Mr. Bloom announced public approval: "I like vocabulary!" Mrs. Moskowitz even prepared her notebook without a single prophetic "Oy!" Young Mr. Nathan chuckled. And Mr. Kaplan opened his box of crayons, smiled a solar smile, turned to a fresh page in his notebook and, long before Mr. Parkhill even reached his name in the alphabetical roll, printed:

*VOCAPULARY*
(Prectice in Book. Then Go to Blackb. and putting on.)
by
*H\*Y\*M\*A\*N   K\*A\*P\*L\*A\*N*

Mr. Parkhill called off the words: "Mr. Blattberg: 'sugar . . . camera . . . breakfast. . . .' Mr. Bloom: 'bicycle . . . delicious . . . policeman. . . .' "

The beginners' grade heaved into action. Brows furrowed, chins were stroked, heads scratched, dictionaries riffled. "Mr. Kaplan, your words are: 'pitcher . . . fascinate . . . university.' "

Mr. Parkhill noticed that Mr. Kaplan's thinking process involved closing one eye, cocking his head to one side, pronouncing each word to himself, then, emerging from his interior caucus, testing the word in a sentence in a whisper that could be heard with ease anywhere in the room. " 'Pitcher . . . pitcher . . .' " Mr. Kaplan murmured. "Is maybe a pitcher for *milk*? Could be. . . . Is maybe a pitcher on de vall? Also could be. Aha! So is *two* minninks! Exemples: 'Plizz put milk in de pitcher.' Or 'De pitcher hengs cockeye.' "

Suddenly it dawned on Mr. Parkhill that Mr. Kaplan's soliloquy was not a mannerism but a stratagem: for as he murmured a sentence with one eye closed, he watched Mr. Parkhill out of the eye that was open. The man was trying to discern from his teacher's expressions which interpretation of "pitcher" would be acceptable! Mr. Parkhill froze his features into neutrality.

Soon, four students trooped to the blackboard, transcribed their sentences and returned to their seats. When Mr. Kaplan finished his three sentences, he glanced proudly toward Mr. Parkhill (who, pretending to scruti-

144

nize the blackboard, was unconsciously watching Mr. Kaplan out of the corner of *his* eye) and hurried to the front of the room.

"Well," said Mr. Parkhill after the boards could take no more chalking, "let's start at—er—this end. Mr. Bloom."

Norman Bloom read his sentences with crisp authority.

1. She needs a *bicicle*.
2. The soup is *delicious*.
3. Last Saturday, I found a *policeman*.

"Excellent!" said Mr. Parkhill. "Are there any questions?"

There were no questions.

"Any—uh—*corrections*? . . . Mr. Bloom spelled one word incorrectly."

There were no corrections either. So Mr. Parkhill changed "bicicle" to "bicycle," pointing out the amusing difference between a cycle and an icicle. ("My!" Mr. Kaplan exclaimed.) The exercise marched on.

On the whole, things went surprisingly well. Except for young Mr. Nathan's misuse of "chorus" ("She sings in the school chores") and Mr. Blattberg's unfortunate twisting of "tan" ("one, two, three . . . nine, tan"), the students' sentences were quite good. Vocabulary was proving a decided success.

"Next . . . Mr. Kaplan."

Mr. Kaplan rose. "Mine foist void, ladies an' gantleman an' Mr. Pockheel"—Mr. Kaplan would be crushed if denied his introductory fanfare—"is 'pitcher.' I am usink it in dis santence: 'Oh, how beauriful is dis pitcher.' "

Mr. Parkhill hesitated. "Er—Mr. Kaplan, the word I gave you was 'pi*tch*er,' not 'pi*c*ture.' "

"Mr. Pockheel, dis void *is*—"

"No, no. When you say, 'Oh, how *beautiful*' are you not in fact talking about a pi*c*ture?!"

145

Mr. Kaplan consulted his Muse. "If you *pay* enough for a pitcher it's as beauriful—"

Mr. Parkhill winced. He had been gulled: Hyman Kaplan had straddled both words through a canny use of one. "Read your next sentence."

"De sacond void," declaimed Hyman Kaplan, "is 'fessinate'—an' believe me dat is a planty hod void! So is mine santence: 'In Hindia, is all kinds snake fessinators.'"

"You are thinking of snake *charmers*," said Mr. Parkhill.

"Snek *'chommers'*? In mine dictionary I couldn't find 'fessin—'"

"That's probably because it's spelled with an 's-c-,'" Mr. Parkhill explained; and (before anyone could blurt "Why?") went on: "Suppose you try the word in another sentence. 'Fascinate' in its active sense means to attract, to interest greatly; or, if one *is* fascinated, it means to *be* intensely interested or attracted to . . ."

"Hau Kay." Mr. Kaplan took thought and said, "You fessinate me."

Mr. Parkhill asked Mr. Kaplan to read his last sentence.

"Mine toid void is 'univoisity.'"

"That should be 'my'—not 'mine'—'th*ir*d w*or*d is univ*er*sity'!"

But Mr. Kaplan had already launched into his crowning sentence: "'Elaven yiss dey are married, so is time for de tvalft univoisity.'"

"Mistake!" chirped Miss Mitnick. "Mr. Kaplan mixes up two words. He means *'anni*versary,' which comes each year. But 'university' is a college—the highest college!"

"Good for Rose Mitnick!" called Miss Pomeranz.

"Very good, Miss Mitnick," said Mr. Parkhill. "Do you see the difference, Mr. Kaplan?"

Mr. Kaplan, who had listened to Miss Mitnick with courtly sufferance, wrinkled his nose.

"Try another sentence using 'university.' "

"Som pipple didn't have iven vun day's aducation in a *uni*voisity"—Mr. Kaplan's glance at Miss Mitnick was withering—"but still, efter elaven yiss marritch dey have deir tvalft *an*nivoisery!"

Miss Mitnick bit her lip. Mr. Nathan winked at her, with some effect.

"Keplen never sorrenders!" crowed Mr. Pinsky.

"He never gives an *inch!*" wailed Bessie Shimmelfarb.

"Oy!" scowled Mrs. Moskowitz.

"Next student."

Throughout the remaining recitations, Mr. Kaplan sat strangely silent. He did not bother to comment on Mrs. Yanoff's spectacular misuse of "guess" ("Turn off the guess"). He did not so much as take a side-swipe at Carmen Caravello's unfortunate use of "omit" ("The child omits a cry"). He let pass even Casimir Scymczak's egregious use of "hoarse" ("He hollers until his troat feels like a horse").

Throughout the lively discussion each of these solecisms triggered, Mr. Kaplan kept a cryptic smile glued to his lips. It was obvious that in his sensitive soul smoldered the memory of humiliation at the hands of Rose Mitnick.

Mr. Parkhill felt uneasy. "Miss Mitnick, I believe you are last . . ."

Miss Mitnick rose, blushing, and in a tremulous timbre read: " '*Enamel* is used for painting chairs.' "

Out rang Mr. Kaplan's voice: "Mistake by Mitnick!" It was more like a battlecry than a notification. "Ha! Mit *enimals* she is painting chairs?! Mit monkeys—or pussycets—"

"The word is 'e*na*mel'!" said Mr. Parkhill, severely. "Not '*a*nimal.' Miss Mitnick is absolutely right."

Mr. Kaplan looked as if he had been stabbed in the back.

"Good for Miss Mitnick," laughed Mr. Vinograd.

"Shame, shame, Mr. Koplon!"

So profound was Mr. Kaplan's mortification that he allowed Miss Mitnick's reading of her next sentences to go unchallenged. (There was, in truth, little anyone *could* challenge in Miss Mitnick's, "Oh, how men are selfish in every *century.*" Or in her wistful, "I wish I could play any *piano.*")

Miss Mitnick's final sentence was a *tour de force:* "In English movies, we see that the prisoner stands in a courts *dock.*"

"Mistake by Mitnick!" cried Mr. Kaplan.

Mr. Parkhill tried to head him off. "There should be a certain punctuation mark, Miss Mitnick, in 'courts.' . . ."

"Dat's not my mistake!" Mr. Kaplan was aggrieved.

"I—" flushed Miss Mitnick. "I—forgot to put the apostrophe betwin 't' and 's'!"

"Exactly!" Mr. Parkhill chalked the sign of the possessive. "Very good, Miss Mitnick."

*"Still* not my mistake!" declared Mr. Kaplan. "De void 'dock' is used wronk!"

"Not at all! Miss Mitnick has used 'dock' in one of its perfectly proper uses. In England, those accused of a crime do stand on a raised platform, which is popularly called the—er—'dock.' "

"I am t'inkink abot Americans."

"Well, Mr. Kaplan, there *is* a more—familiar American usage. Can you use 'dock' that way, Miss Mitnick?"

Miss Mitnick floundered in cerebration.

Miss Ziev went to the ladies' room.

"Anyone . . . ?" asked Mr. Parkhill.

"I like roast dock," said Mr. Kaplan.

"No, no, no! That word is 'd*u*ck'! There is all the difference in the *world,* Mr. Kaplan, between a 'dock' and a 'duck'!" Mr. Parkhill placed "dock" and "duck" on the board with a decisiveness that matched his speed. "You *see* how important enunciation is, class? Mr. Kaplan is confusing the 'u' sound with the 'o' sound—just as he does when he pronounces 'bog' as—er—'bug'! If we learn to speak carefully, we will be helped to spell correctly. And vice versa!"

Mr. Kaplan looked woebegone. Mr. Marcus looked blissful.

"Notice once more the word I gave Miss Mitnick. It is not a hard word, class." Mr. Parkhill tapped each letter with his pointer. " 'D-o-c-k' . . . Now, anyone?"

Anyone, alas, became no one.

"Let me give you a hint, class. Each of you, in coming to America, had *direct experience with a dock.*" Mr. Parkhill paused. "Now is that clearer? *Think,* class."

The class fell into a frenzied search of memory. (Mrs. Moskowitz, reliving her seasickness, searched no further.) Mr. Perez scratched his scalp to stimulate his powers of recall. Miss Goldberg enlisted the aid of a piece of peanut brittle. Mr. Pinsky, who was scanning a comic book, made no response at all. And Mr. Kaplan, desperate to make the dramatic, redeeming kill, rummaged through his associations in frantic whisperings: " 'Dock' . . . Commink to America . . . old boat . . . big wafes . . . seeink lend. . . ."

They were getting nowhere. Miss Kipnis kept wrinkling her brow in vain. Oscar Trabish had slid into slumber. Mr. Norman Bloom apparently forgot all about "dock" (he was, in fact, recalling a pinochle game on the S.S. *Potovski,* in which he had won four and a half dollars) and mopped his bald dome.

"I'll make it even easier," blurted Mr. Parkhill. "Where did your boats land?"

"Alice Island!" beamed Hyman Kaplan.

Mr. Parkhill frowned. "You landed at *E*llis, not *A*lice, Island. But in discussing the word 'dock' *I* meant specifically—"

An ululation of pure joy ascended. "I got him! Ufcawss!

149

'Dock!' Plain an' tsimple! Ha!" Mr. Kaplan shot a scathing arrow at Rose Mitnick. "I'm soprise a student like Mitnick shouldn't know a plain void like 'dock.' I got de enswer! Mr. Pockheel—"

How Mr. Parkhill wished that some other student—any other student—would volunteer. His glance swept the ranks. "Miss Valuskas?"

Miss Valuskas looked limp.

"Mrs.—Shimmelfarb?"

Mrs. Shimmelfarb looked haggard.

"Mr. Matsoukas?"

Mr. Gus Matsoukas was totally deaf to Mr. Parkhill's words; he seemed hypnotized by Mr. Kaplan's hand, which was wig-wagging like a metronome.

Mr. Parkhill confronted the inevitable. "Very well . . . Mr. Kaplan."

The man from "Alice Island" said, "Hello, *Doc*!"

Even while shaking his head frostily to inform Mr. Kaplan that he had gone wildly astray once more, Mr. Parkhill thought, "Vocabulary. Above all, we *must* increase their vocabulary!"

# 14

## CAPTAIN K·A·P·L·A·N

Mr. Parkhill was not at all surprised when the first three students delivered orations on "Abraham Lincoln," "Little George and the Sherry Tree," and "Wonderful America," respectively. During the month of February, the classrooms of the American Night Preparatory School for Adults throbbed with patriotic fervor, and the passionate *amor patriae* usually welled well into March.

The cause was simple: Mr. Robinson, the school principal, could never allow the birthdays of Lincoln and Washington to pass uncelebrated. On each of these hallowed occasions, the entire student body crowded into Franklin Hall (that Benjamin Franklin's nativity went uncommemorated was something Mr. Parkhill always deplored) for a solemn ceremony.

At the Lincoln assembly, each year, Mr. Robinson delivered a tribute entitled "The Great Emancipator." ("His name is inscribed on the tablet of history, in letters of eternal gold!") After that, the star student from the senior class delivered a pithy oration, which Mrs. O'Hallohan had edited. Then Miss Higby recited Walt Whitman's "O Captain! My Captain!" No one could elocute "O Captain! My Captain!" the way Miss Higby did, and each time she finished, the students shook Franklin's walls with their ovation.

For the Washington convocation, the order of things was much the same: Mr. Robinson's address was entitled "The Immortal Father of Our Country." ("First in war, first in peace, first in the hearts of his countrymen—yes, but far more than that! His name will forever burn in the hearts of true Americans, old *or* new, a glowing ember, a glorious reminder of his deathless achievement!") The star student's speech usually eulogized "Crossing the Delaware" or mourned "The Terrible Winter at Valley Forge." Then Mr. Krout would recite the words of "The Star-Spangled Banner" in his most solemn manner. The ceremony ended with faculty and students together singing "My Country, 'Tis of Thee."

So dramatic were these rites that for weeks afterward, each year, every teacher in the A.N.P.S.A. was deluged with essays on Lincoln or Washington, speeches on the Gettysburg Address or the Declaration of Independence, even poems, odes and ditties on Lincoln *and* Washington. Night after night, the classrooms echoed the historic phrases: "1776," "Honest Abe," "Bunker Hill." Miss Schnepfe, Mr. Robinson's assistant, dubbed the annual rites "The Ides of February and March." (Sixteen years under Mr. Robinson certainly had sharpened Louella Schnepfe's wit.)

Now, a full week after the successive convocations, the beginners' grade still luxuriated in tributes to their new-found heroes. The next-to-last student to face the class was Carmen Caravello. "I will spik ona man joosta lak Georgio Washington—great Giuseppe Garibaldi!"

After the torrent of benisons to Washington and Lincoln, Mr. Parkhill felt a surge of relief. It was short-lived.

"Garibaldi! Firsta in war, also in peace, *per primo* in da heartsa alla countryman!"

The scholars scarcely stirred. They were sated. Wolfgang Schmitt twiddled his thumbs. "Cookie" Kipnis dipped into Miss Goldberg's cache of "monkey nuts," Mr.

Trabish dozed so thoroughly that he might just as well have been in Mexico.

"Eacha letter isa *burn* (lak Mist' Robinson say): da 'g,' da 'a,' da 'r,' da 'i' . . ." Miss Caravello articulated the letters of Sicily's liberator with zeal. Mrs. Yanoff yawned.

Mr. Parkhill noticed that Mr. Kaplan, on his preempted throne in the center of the front row, had been sighing, twitching, coughing or snorting throughout the preceding orations. That was odd. For Mr. Kaplan to display ennui where Washington and Lincoln were concerned boded no good; Mr. Kaplan was yet to deliver his own ruminations.

"Anda I find out thata Giuseppe Garibaldi, *Comandante* of *Cacciatori delle Alpi,* he liveda here ina U.S.!"

Mr. Kaplan sat up, narrowing both eyes.

"He wasa working asa maker ofa candles!"

Mr. Kaplan's eyebrows doubled his disbelief.

"Anda I find out Garibaldi—wasa *citizen U.S.A.!* So— Horray, Georgio Washington! *Viva* Giuseppe Garibaldi! *Viva, viva, viva!"* With that triple display of chauvinism, Carmen Caravello flounced back to her seat.

Miss Mitnick breathed, "Oh, Carmen!"

Nathan P. Nathan patted the breathless eulogist on the back, but winked, renewing fealty, at Miss Mitnick.

*"Da, da,"* moaned Olga Tarnova. "We should more respact great mon from *all* nations . . ."

"Thank you, Miss Caravello," said Mr. Parkhill. "That was very—thought-provoking. . . . Now, class, comments . . . ?"

Karl Finsterwald cited Miss Caravello's customary garbling of the past and present tenses. Gerta Valuskas criticized Miss Caravello's habit of attaching melodious "a"s right and left to English words which recoiled from them. Harry Feigenbaum suggested with steely rectitude that the proper phrasing was "foist *in* war, foist *in* peace, foist *in* the hearts his countrymen."

153

"Correct . . . right . . . quite so," said Mr. Parkhill. "Any more?"

The scornful tenor of Hyman Kaplan sliced through the air. "How can enybody compare a Judge Vashington mit a Gary Baldy? Ha!"

"Fathers of a country are alla same!" retorted Miss Caravello. "Heroes! Greata men!"

*"Candy* makers?" leered Mr. Kaplan.

" 'Can*dle,'* Mr. Kaplan, not 'can*dy'!"* Mr. Parkhill hastily intervened. "Miss Caravello happens to be right. It is a little-known fact that Garibaldi did work as a candlemaker . . . Any further comments? Very well; our final speaker is—Mr. Kaplan."

"Can't we skip him?" hissed Mr. Bloom, *sotto voce.*

"Oy," agreed Mrs. Moskowitz, *a priori.*

"Never!" cried Mr. Pinsky, *con brio.*

Deaf to both foe and friend, Mr. Kaplan strode frontwards. He turned to the divided tribunes, delicately buttoned his coat, made a slight bow to Mr. Parkhill, shot his cuffs and sang out: "Fallow petriots!" He paused for a fraction of a moment. "Judge Vashington! Abram Lincohen! Jake Popper!"

"Er—Mr. Kaplan," said Mr. Parkhill anxiously, *"please* watch your pronunciation. It's *'George'* not *'Judge'* 'Washington,' not 'Vashington.' And 'Abra*ham* Lin*coln,'* not 'Abram Lin*cohen.'* " (Mr. Parkhill could think of nothing to say about Jake Popper, of whom he had never heard.)

"Hau Kay," conceded Hyman Kaplan. "So foist abot *Jaw*dge *Wa*shington. Ve—we all know abot his movvellous didds. How, beink a leetle boy, he chopped off all de cherries on a tree so he could ensswer, 'I kennot tell a lie, Papa. I did it mit mine leetle hatchek.' "

" 'Hat*chet,'* not 'hat-*check'!"*

"Hat*chet.* . . . But ve shouldn't forgat more important

154

fects abot dis vunderful hero! *Jaw*dge *W*ashington vas a ravolutionist, fightink for friddom, friddom against de very bed Kink of England—"

" '*Kin*g—' "

"—Kin*g* Jawdge Number Tree, dat no-goot autocrap who—"

" 'Auto*crat*'!" Mr. Parkhill was aghast.

"—who vas iven puddink stemps on *tea,* so it tasted tarrible! An' *Jaw*dge *W*ashington trew dat whole bunch tea in de vater fromm Boston Hobber, but he vas smot so he drassed op like a Hindian!"

"He was *not* in Boston, nor disguised as—" Mr. Parkhill might as well have been addressing a Zulu. The entire class hung on to Mr. Kaplan's orison: even vengeful Bloom, sullen Tarnova, prickly Blattberg—all seemed hypnotized by Mr. Kaplan's dramatic revision of history.

"My! Vas Jawdge a hero. Foist-cless! . . . Vun night in de meedle a frizzing vinter, he lad his loyal soldiers across de ice in a canoe—"

"*Mr.* Kap—"

"—because he knew he vould cetch de British an' all deir missionaries—"

" '*Mercen*aries'!"

"—foolink arond, not mit deir minds on duty! So *W*ashington von de var!"

" '*W*on the *w*ar!' " loud and clear went unheeded.

"So de pipple sad, 'Jawdge, you our hero! Our rill lidder! Ve love you! You should live till a hondrit an' tvanty yiss old! Ve elact you Prazident de whole U.S.A.' So he vas elacted—anonymously—"

Mr. Parkhill's " 'Un*an*imously' " drowned in the rolling wave of words.

"—an' like Mr. Robinson sad, before de whole school, 'In *W*ashington's name is itch ladder like a hot piece coal, boinink ot his gloryous achivmants!' " Mr. Kaplan embroi-

155

dered the achievements with an imperial sweep of his arm.

"You *must* speak more slowly," protested Mr. Parkhill. (He could not forget that Lincoln and "Jake Popper" were yet to come.)

"I'll try." The noble sigh, the gracious inclination of the head—who could deny that though Hyman Kaplan's body was in the beginners' grade, his soul was in Carnegie Hall? "So now I toin to Abra*ham* Lincollen. Vat a human man. Vat a naubel cherecter. Vat a hot—like *gold!* Look, look!" Mr. Kaplan flung a finger toward the wall where a lithograph of the Great Emancipator reposed. "Look on dat sveet face! Look on dose ice, so sed mit fillink. Obsoive his mot, so full goodness. See his high forehat—showink tremandous *brens!*" Mr. Kaplan's searing glance at Miss Caravello suggested that brains were not Garibaldi's strong point. "Look on dat honest axpression! I esk you: Is it a vunder averybody called him 'Honest Abie'?"

" 'Honest Abe'!" Nathan P. Nathan laughed like a hyena.

The Cicero of the beginners' grade answered his own question. "No, it's no vunder. Lincollen vas a poor boy, a voodchopper, a rail-splitter. But he made de Tsivil Var." (Mr. Parkhill wiped his dampening brow.) "Oh, my, den came terrible times! Shoodink, killink, de Naut Site U.S. aganst de Sot Site U.S. Blecks aganst vhites, brodder fightink brodder . . . An' who von? *Who?* Ha! Abraham Lincollen!" Thrice did Kaplan nod. "So he decidet all bleck pipple should be exectly like vhite! Ufcawss, Lincollen couldn't change deir collars—"

" '*Col*ors,' not—"

"—de blecks still stayt bleck. But *free* bleck, not slafe bleck! Citizens, not kettle. Americans, true-blue, no metter how bleck. An' Lincollen gave ot de Mancipation Prockilmation: 'All men are born an' createt in de same vay!' So he vas killed!"

156

Mr. Kaplan paused, heavy of heart and funereal in manner. The eyes of Fanny Gidwitz glazed before him. The eyes of Sam Pinsky shone star-struck. Rochelle Goldberg fumbled for a gumdrop.

"So maybe you vonderink, 'Vat's all dis got to do mit Jake Popper?'" Their expressions testified to the fact that Mr. Kaplan had taken the question right out of his colleagues' mouths. "I'll axplain. Jake Popper also vas a fine man, like Abe Lincollen, mit a hot like gold. Ve called him 'Honest Jake.'"

Mr. Schmitt began to strangle.

"Jake Popper vasn't a beeg soldier like *W*ashington. He didn't make a Valley Fudge—"

"'*For*ge'!"

"—or free any slafes. . . . Jake Popper owned a dalicatessen. An' in dat store the poorest pipple, pipple mitout a panny, could alvays gat somting to itt."

"'*Eat*'!"

"Jake Popper vas ebsolutely a frand to de poor. He did a fine business—on cradit. So averybody loved him . . . Vun day, Honest Jake vas fillink vary bed. He had hot an' cold vaves on de body by de same time—vat doctors call a fivver—"

"'F*e*ver!'" pleaded Mr. Parkhill.

"—so averybody said, 'Jake, lay don in your bat, take it izzy, rast. But did Honest Jake lay don in his bat? Did he take it izzy—"

"'*Ea*sy.'"

"—an' rast? Not Jake Popper! He stood brave behind de conter in dat delicatessen, day an' night. He said, 'I got to soive mine customers!' Dat's de high sanse *duty* he had!" Whether from throat strain or emotion, hoarseness entered Mr. Kaplan's voice. "Oh, sed, sed, sed, to play mit halth for de sek of odders. . . . So dey had to call a doctor, and he came an' said, 'Mr. Popper, you got bronxitis!' So

157

Jake vent into his bat. An' got *more* seeck. So de foist doctor insulted odder doctors—"

"You mean *'con*sulted'—"

"—an' dey took him to Mont Sinus Hospital—"

" 'Mount Sinai'!"

"—vhere dey fond Jake Popper had double demonia! So dey gave him spacial noises—"

" *'Nurses'*!"

"—an' from all kinds madicine de bast, iven oxenjin tants, he should be able to breed. An' dey gave him blood confusions—"

" *'Transf*usions'!"

"—an' dey shot him in de arm he should fall aslip, mit epidemics. An' efter three long dace and nights, Honest Jake Popper pest avay." The mention of death brought a hush sufficient to turn the classroom into a cemetery. Miss Mitnick lowered her head. Mr. Nathan tried to look glum. Mrs. Rodriguez fingered her crucifix. "So in Jake Popper's honor I'll recite a pome—like Miss Hikby did de same vit 'O Ceptin, my Ceptin!' " Mr. Kaplan lifted a paper from his pocket, raised both his head and the sheet high, and, as Mr. Parkhill sought solace in the ceiling, declaimed this benediction:

> "O hot! hot! hot!
> O de bliddink drops rad!
> Dere on de dack
> Jake Popper lies,
> Fallink cold an' dad!"

Celestial wings fluttered over the American Night Preparatory School for Adults; unseen angels mourned the grandeur that was Popper.

"Isn't dat beauriful?" sighed Mr. Kaplan.

Mr. Parkhill managed to find his voice. "Thank you, Mr.—"

But Mr. Kaplan was adding, "Vun ting more, so de cless shouldn't fill *too* bed abot Jake Popper. It's awreddy nine yiss since he pest avay!"

An invading giraffe would have caused no greater sensation.

*"Hanh?!"* howled Karl Finsterwald.

"Nine *year?!*" shouted Gus Matsoukas.

"Gentlemen—"

"Cookie" Kipnis shot Mr. Kaplan the furious look of one whose emotions had been cruelly exploited. Mr. Scymczak resorted to a Polish oath. Olga Tarnova moaned, "This mon . . . this *mon!*" Young Nathan was beating his thighs in glee.

"An' I didn't go to de funeral." With this extraordinary addendum, Hyman Kaplan, head bent in mourning, returned to his seat.

The class was in an uproar. They bellowed, they hooted, they protested a climax which negated all that had preceded it.

"He didn't went to *funeral?!*" Mrs. Yanoff could not believe anyone so cold-hearted.

"Oooy!"

"He did not even attand the soivices?!" boomed Mr. Bloom.

"I complain!" complained Mr. Perez.

"Class—"

"A shame, a scendel!"

"An insult to the dead!"

"Order, *please*—"

Mr. Blattberg's outrage was so great that it paralyzed his larynx, but this did not prevent him from twirling his gold chain with such vehemence that his grandson's baby tooth struck Miss Schneiderman on the elbow.

Suddenly Miss Valuskas demanded, *"Why you didn't go to the funeral?!"*

"Yas!"

"Enswer!"

"Som frand!"

"This is one excuse I'm dying—excuse the expression—to hear," bubbled Mr. Nathan.

*"Class!* I think—"

No one ever heard what Mr. Parkhill thought, for Mr. Kaplan had risen, stilling the carpers with one tolerant hand. "You all right to esk. Bot connsider de rizzon." His face was a study in both humility and nobility. "Jake Popper's funeral vas in de meedle of de veek. I sad to minesalf, 'Keplen, to go or not to go? Dat is de qvastion. Remamber, you are in America. So *t'ink* like an American!' So I t'ought. An' I didn't go, because I remambered dat fine Yenkee provoib: 'Business bafore plashure!' "

Pandemonium availed the mob nothing.

# 15

## THE FEARFUL VENGEANCE
## OF H·Y·M·A·N  K·A·P·L·A·N

Mr. Parkhill wondered whether he had not been a bit rash vis-à-vis idioms. Idioms are, obviously, of crucial importance in English—or in any other language, for that matter. Was it not Aristotle who called idioms the very foundation of style? . . . Good style, Mr. Parkhill reflected sadly, was a distant dream for the beginners' grade; but idioms—idioms were an immediate necessity and an obstacle to progress.

As Plaut and Samish had so well put it:

Idioms present a particularly difficult challenge to the teacher of English, since they are expressions, often colloquial, whose meaning may differ radically from the meanings of the separate words they employ. Hence, idioms may be both peculiar and exasperating to foreigners unfamiliar with their uniqueness.

Small wonder, then, that Mr. Parkhill had come to regard the idiom as a perverse creature, a goblin who played hob with his students' comprehension. "Is there anyone whose heart does not sink upon first encountering an idiom in a new tongue?" Mr. Parkhill once blurted to Miss Higby. "Why, idioms are like messages in code!"

"Coded messages?" Miss Higby had given him an odd look. "I never thought of it that way. . . ."

But a conscientious teacher *had* to think of it that way. How else explain "She gave him the cold shoulder"? Or "He walked me off my feet"? Or (Great Scott!) "He's going to the dogs"? The more he thought of it, the more Mr. Parkhill saw no way of postponing a lesson on idioms any longer.

So it was that on this gloomy, windswept night, he spent fifteen full minutes explaining to the beginners' grade what idioms are, how they grow, how they convey special, vivid ideas. He had illustrated his lecture with many a fascinating example. And now his students were going to the board, in groups of five, to transcribe the assignment: "Three short sentences, using an idiom in each."

The exercise was not proving altogether successful. Try though Mr. Parkhill did to gloss over the facts, he could not deny that idioms teetered on the brink of disaster.

Mr. Marcus, for example, had adorned the slate with:

It will cost you free.

That, to Mr. Marcus, was an idiom.

Mrs. Tomasic had submitted only one sentence, so depleted was her morale by the complexity of the assignment:

Honestly is the best policy.

Mr. Vincente Perez was groping in the right *direction*, at least, when he concocted:

By 2 in the PM the job will be as good as down.

But Carmen Caravello had been driven delirious, it would seem, by idiom's drastic demands. How else explain:

162

Dont beet donkeys
Dont beet monkeys.
Dont hit babys (or members of family!)

Yes, it had been a trying—a most disappointing—night for Mr. Parkhill. He braced himself to confront the homework to the right of Miss Caravello's. Three lines loomed before him under a sort of marquee:

### 3 SENT. AND IDIOTS
by
H*Y*M*A*N  K*A*P*L*A*N

"Mr. *Kap*lan," said Mr. Parkhill, in horror, "the word is 'idioms,' not 'idiots'!" With uncharacteristic severity, he wiped IDIOTS off the slate and printed IDIOMS in its stead.

"My!" beamed Mr. Kaplan. "Som difference fromm vun lettle latter."

"There certainly is—as we have seen in many of our spelling drills. Why, just recall the consequences of misusing one *vowel,* in the test I gave the class Wednesday."

Up went the hand of Mr. Matsoukas. "I was not here Weddnesday. What was?"

Mr. Parkhill studied his chalk for a moment. "The exercise showed how important it is to watch every letter in your spelling; for one change, one addition, can make a world of difference." He cleared his throat. "I shall not be able to repeat *all* of last Wednesday's drill—"

"I work overtime Weddnesday," muttered Mr. Matsoukas.

"—but here are several examples." In a clear space on the board, Mr. Parkhill wrote:

sat
set
seat

163

sit
sot

"I theenk a nicer example ees 'hat,' " announced Mrs. Rodriguez.

"Very well." Mr. Parkhill wrote a column parallel to the one he had just completed:

hat
heat
hot
hoot
hit
hut

*"My* faworite was 'batter'!" chirped Miss Ziev.

"Yes," Mr. Parkhill nodded, "that *was* an effective example," and he wrote:

batter
better
bitter
biter
butter

"Good lesson," grunted Mr. Matsoukas.

"Good? It vas voit a million dollis!"

"Thank you, Mr. Kaplan. For more examples, see pages eighty-one through eighty-four of our text, Mr. Matsoukas. And I suspect we shall find similar—er—errors as we go along . . . Now, Mr. Kaplan, please read us your idioms."

Mr. Kaplan rose. "Ladies an' gentleman an' Mr. Pockheel. T'ree santences I vas wridink—"

"Can't you even *read* without a speech to Congress?" demanded Mr. Blattberg.

"—on de bleckboard." (Mr. Blattberg lived in limbo, as far as Mr. Kaplan was concerned.) "I tried in dis axercise to—"

Mr. Parkhill tapped the blackboard with his pointer.

"You—there is nothing to *explain,* Mr. Kaplan. Just read your sentences."

"I back your podden," sighed the penitent. "So—mine foist santence . . ." Mr. Kaplan read it:

1. He's nots.

Mr. Nathan fell off his chair.

Mr. Parkhill adjusted his glasses. "That is *not* an idiom, Mr. Kaplan. That's—slang."

The paling of his rosy features left no doubt that Mr. Kaplan had put his heart and soul into "He's nots."

"He's nots!" crowed Mr. Bloom. (It wasn't clear whether he was mocking Mr. Kaplan's sentence or describing his mental condition.)

"Ve hear many pipple usink dose exect voids!" Mr. Kaplan protested.

"It does not matter how many people say it, Mr. Kaplan. Besides, you spelled the word—er—'nuts' wrong."

"I dit?"

"It's 'n-*u*-t-s,' not 'n-*o*-t-s.' " Mr. Parkhill printed N-U-T-S on the board. "There, Mr. Matsoukas, is an excellent example of what I was stressing just a moment ago!"

Mr. Kaplan looked mortified. "Mine sacond santence. . . ." The second sentence was, if anything, more astonishing than the first:

2. Get the jams. By hook or cook!

"Is that English or Chinese?" jeered Mr. Blattberg.

"I think Mr. Kaplan meant 'gems,' not 'jams.' " Mr. Parkhill erased the latter and wrote the former.

" 'Jem' is for puttink on brat!" crowed Mrs. Moskowitz. "A 'gem' is for charity bells—"

" '*Balls,*' Mrs. Moskowitz. But let us get back to the idiom. 'By hook or cook' is *almost* correct, but—class, what is wrong?"

"Should be 'by hook *and* cook!' " sallied Miss Goldberg.

"That," said Mr. Parkhill glumly, "would only make it worse."

Miss Goldberg revived herself with a Life Saver.

"I think it should be, 'By hook or *crook*,'" blushed Miss Mitnick—at Mr. Nathan.

"Exactly! Thank you, Miss Mitnick. . . . *'Crook,'* Mr. Kaplan, not 'cook.'"

"I t'ought a 'crook' is a boiglar—"

"*'Bur*glar.'"

"—a chitter—"

"*'Cheat*er,' Mr. Kap—"

"—a plain, low-don tiff!"

"'Thief'!" Mr. Parkhill's throat was getting dry. "The word 'crook' can mean any—or all—of those things; but the phrase 'by hook or by crook' means to use any means whatsoever to—er—get the gems."

"Iven like a crook!"

"But you wrote *'cook,'* Mr. Kaplan, not 'crook'!"

Mr. Kaplan cocked his head. "Som cooks are crooks, an' some crooks are cooks."

*"Mein Gott!"* howled Wolfgang Schmitt.

"Don't choppa hairs!" flashed Miss Caravello.

"He *kills* me!" gasped Nathan P. Nathan.

"Mr. Kaplan"—Mr. Parkhill was wrestling with both astonishment and displeasure—"read your last sentence."

Mr. Kaplan read it with alacrity:

3. Hang yoursalf in reseption hall, please.

"God's almighty!" whooped Norman Bloom, which triggered a giggle from Miss Gidwitz and a guffaw from Mr. Vinograd.

*"Koplan* ees nuts!" laughed Vincente Perez. "Weeth a 'u'!"

"Class . . ."

"Read that idiom again!" grinned "Cookie" Kipnis. "I love it!"

"Heng — yoursalf — in — resaption — hall — plizz," stout Kaplan repeated.

"I dun't be*lieve* it!" cackled Miss Pomeranz.

"I *do*," leered Mr. Finsterwald.

"Oy," oyed Mrs. Moskowitz.

Above these savage indictments, Mr. Parkhill managed to call, "Class, quiet! . . . Mr. Kaplan, examine that sentence carefully. Pay special attention to the object of the verb 'hang' and you will see why the sentence struck the class as being so—funny."

"Hmmnh." Mr. Kaplan pursed his lips, wrinkled his brow, closed one eye, and searched for the treacherous source of his colleagues' pleasure.

*"Nu,* Kaplan?" gibed Norman Bloom.

"Aha! Should be kepitals on 'resaption hall'!"

The Bloom-Moskowitz-Blattberg entente rocked in rapture: "Cuckoo!" "Absoid!" "Som gass!"

"No, Mr. Kaplan," said Mr. Parkhill, " 'reception hall' is not a proper noun, hence does not require capital letters. It is the *meaning* of your sentence that's at fault. 'Hang *yourself* in the reception hall,' Mr. Kaplan? Is that—er— what you say to your guests?"

"I try to make mine gasts fill at home."

Mr. Bloom brayed, " 'Hang *yoursalf*'? Som host!"

"If soitin pipple came to mine house," murmured Hyman Kaplan, "dat vould be exectly vhat I vould say!"

"Oy!"

"Shame!"

Mr. Nathan was in hysterics.

*"Mr.* Kaplan!"

When only ten minutes remained in the night's allotted span, Mr. Parkhill put the class through a vigorous spelling drill. (Of all time fillers, spelling drills were the safest.) "Restaurant . . ."

The class inscribed varying versions of "restaurant" on

the pages before them—all of the class, that is, except Mr. Kaplan. He wrote nothing. He sat with his arms folded.

"Chocolate . . ."

Lids lowered, Mr. Kaplan retreated into that inner world in which his steadfast Muse resided.

"Bungalow," called Mr. Parkhill.

Mr. Kaplan might just as well have retired to a monastery.

"Accident . . . skip . . . lettuce . . ."

Mr. Kaplan opened his eyes. On the pad before him, he now crayonned aimless scribbles and scratches, doodles and hatches.

"Shampoo . . ."

A faint smile formed on Mr. Kaplan's lips.

"Mystery . . ."

Mr. Kaplan unscrewed his fountain pen. He was humming.

"B-basement . . ." Mr. Parkhill faltered.

Mr. Kaplan propelled his pen across the paper with startling speed.

"Hurricane . . ."

Mr. Kaplan chuckled, dotting an "i," crossing a "t."

With but a moment remaining before the large hand on the clock over the door reached 10, Mr. Parkhill announced the last word loudly: "Confess! . . ."

So fleeting, so secretive was Mr. Kaplan's smile that Mr. Parkhill could not help but think of Mona Lisa.

At her post in the principal's office, alert Miss Schnepfe pressed the button which tintinnabulated the final bell.

The students stood up and packed up for their trek home. The room became a sonic jumble of friendly chatter, closing briefcases, snapping rubbers. The class filed past Mr. Parkhill's desk to drop off their exercise papers. "Good night"s—some hearty, some weary—rent the air. Mr. Kaplan's farewell was uncharacteristically blithe: "Ontil ve mit agan . . ."

Mr. Parkhill wiped his hands.

When all had gone, he took his attendance report to Mr. Robinson's office.

"Good attendance?" asked Miss Schnepfe.

"Oh, yes. Only three absent." Hastily, he added, "Mr. Trabish is in the hospital, I believe. Appendicitis."

"Tell him to cut it out!" Miss Schnepfe flung her head back, cackling in glee. (No one enjoyed her own wit more than Miss Schnepfe: Mr. Krout was sure that she tippled.)

"Good night."

It was chilly outside. The city was swathed in bleakness. Mr. Parkhill wrapped his muffler tightly and hurried to the subway.

No sooner did he find a seat than he opened his briefcase and began to scan the pages on which his students had written the spelling test. Miss Mitnick had done *very* well, as usual. Mr. Bloom had managed to scale the heights of an 85! Young Mr. Nathan had outdone himself, except for "shampoo," which, given his athletic inclinations, he had rendered as "champoo." Mr. Scymczak had misspelled only eight out of fifteen words—a superior performance for Casimir Scymczak. Mrs. Moskowitz . . . poor Mrs. Moskowitz; she was still confusing English with some other, unrevealed language.

The next paper was blank. Mr. Parkhill frowned. Some student had turned in an empty page by mistake. Mr. Parkhill turned the paper over, to pass on to the next one, but beheld a conglomeration of scrawls, numbers and tic-tac-toes: there was even an unfinished ear and an American flag, executed in colors. Firmly, Mr. Parkhill wrote on top of the page: "Mr. Kaplan: Please submit your spelling drill!"

He was about to proceed to Miss Caravello's offering, when something caught his eye. Words had been written around those vagrant hieroglyphics. Mr. Parkhill adjusted his glasses and looked closer:

Critsising Mitnick
is a picnick.

Natan P. Natan,
For what are you waitin?

Bloom, Bloom
Go out the room!

Olga Tarnova
Is crazy all over.

Mrs. Moskowitz,
By her it doesn't fits
A dress—size 44.

It was a fearful vengeance which Mr. Kaplan, defeated but unbowed, had wreaked upon those who had tried to besmirch his honor.

# 16

## MR. K·A·P·L·A·N SLASHES A
## GORDIAN KNOT

"Tonight," said Mr. Parkhill, "we come to our semester's end—and thus to our final examination."

It was not really necessary for Mr. Parkhill to go through the formality of a final examination. He well knew, weeks before the end of a term, which members of the beginners' grade deserved to be promoted to Miss Higby's Advanced Grammar and Civics, and which students, by even the most generous measure of achievement, would have to be "held back."

Mr. Parkhill *hated* to hold any student back. The night before a final examination he would toss and turn in bed, trying to justify the possible promotion of "borderline cases": a student such as Mr. Marcus, for example, who had worked very hard, improved his spelling, reformed his grammar, but still deformed his diction. (Asked for an oral sentence using "denounce," Mr. Marcus had burbled, "I have trouble with verbs, but never de nouns.") Or a pupil as wayward as Mrs. Rodriguez, whose Hispanic ear just was not attuned to English sounds. (In one composition, Mrs. Rodriguez had written: "Today, I heard a funny choke.")

Mr. Parkhill often fell asleep only after forcing himself to think about students he could promote without the slightest moral qualms: Miss Mitnick, for example: there was no shred of doubt in Mr. Parkhill's mind that Miss Mitnick was ready for Miss Higby's tutelage. Or Wolfgang Schmitt. True, Mr. Schmitt's pronunciation of "th"s as "zzz"s begged for alteration, yet this in no way affected the excellence of his spelling, the soundness of his syntax, the range of his vocabulary. Mr. Schmitt would surely pass. Or Gerta Valuskas. Why, Miss Valuskas should be ready for *graduation* from the American Night Preparatory School for Adults in several years. Or Nathan P. Nathan. He spoke English so fluently, but played basketball so often; Miss Schnepfe would raise a frightful rumpus over so errant an attendance chart—much more than over Mr. Nathan's aberrant spelling or absent punctuation.

But upon awakening from his slumbers, Mr. Parkhill would go right back to worrying about the pupils he would be forced to disappoint. Mrs. Moskowitz, for example. By no stretch of either hope, faith or charity could Mrs. Moskowitz be given the cherished "Passed." (Only last week, Mrs. Moskowitz had defined "absolute" as "won't salute.")

Or Gus Matsoukas. Mr. Matsoukas's English was as unnerving as his mutterings. In a recent exercise on new words, the immigrant from Greece, given "ponder," had growled, "Every night I clean with toot ponder."

Or Mr. Kaplan. Mr. Parkhill winced. (Mr. Parkhill had come to wince whenever he thought of Hyman Kaplan.) That intrepid scholar was surely the most diligent and determined soul in the class: he never missed a lesson; he never grew discouraged; the smile of optimism, of undaunted aspiration, rarely fled those cherubic features. But Mr. Kaplan's English still shuttled between the barbaric and the unheard of. His spelling remained eccentric, his grammar deplorable, his pronunciation—there was only one word to describe Mr. Kaplan's pronunciation: hair-raising. (Were one to accept Mr. Kaplan's usage, "grin" is a color, "pitch" a fruit, and a "kit" anyone under twenty-one.)

In all fairness, Mr. Parkhill reminded himself, Mr. Kaplan *had* shown commendable improvement in ever so many zones: "because" was certainly an advance over "becawss," and "singink" was certainly better than "sink-ink." But so much of Mr. Kaplan's English remained to *be* improved that the hills of his progress shrank before the mountain of his errors.

One could only marvel over Mr. Kaplan's uncanny capacity to resolve one problem by creating another. On Tuesday, for instance, Mr. Kaplan had implored his classmates to avoid any foods or agitations that cause "high blood pleasure." In an exercise on comparative adjectives, he had submitted, "Cold, colder, below zero." In a quite routine review of gender, Mr. Kaplan had ordained that "opera" was masculine but "operetta" feminine. And (the very recollection made Mr. Parkhill pale) Mr. Kaplan believed that the bravest of American frontiersmen was "Daniel Bloom."

Sometimes Mr. Parkhill wondered whether it wasn't unfair to try to clamp the chains of conformity on so unfettered an intelligence.

The time had come. The last exam was at hand. "Please clear the arms of your chairs of everything except paper, pens or pencils."

Up rose the hand of Mr. Pinsky.

"Yes?"

"Is allowed to hold bladders?"

It took Mr. Parkhill a moment of acute distress to figure out what Mr. Pinsky meant. " '*Blotters*'! Oh, yes, Mr. Pinsky. If you are using ink, you certainly may hold on to your—er—blotters. Is everyone ready?"

Rueful nods, brave smiles, resigned suspirations—all testified to the momentous inquest ahead. Many a mouth went dry; many a heart beat faster. In the eyes of some students glowed visions of Advanced Grammar and Civics;

173

in the eyes of others—well, life had taught them not to elevate their expectations. Down the waiting ranks, pens and pencils poised like falcons. Miss Mitnick's hair was disarranged. Miss Tarnova inhaled a restorative scent from the Orient. Mr. Nathan looked as if he had just put two free throws through the hoop. Miss Goldberg swallowed raisins.

"The first part of our examination will be a combined spelling-vocabulary test," said Mr. Parkhill. "Write a sentence—a short sentence—using each of the words I shall call off. Is that clear?"

The "Oy" of Mrs. Moskowitz suggested that it was too clear.

"Very well . . . Our first word is—'knees.' " Mr. Parkhill paused and repeated, " 'Knees,' " buzzing the terminal fricative as if it were "z."

The class attacked "knees." Mr. Kaplan leaned back, closed his eyes, and sought aid from his guardian angel. " 'Neez,' " he whispered. " 'Neez' . . . a fonny void . . ." He opened one eye to monitor Mr. Parkhill's reaction to the soliloquy yet to come. "Aha! Has *two* minninks. . . . Vun, a piece of a lag. . . . Two, mine sister's daughter is mine nee—"

"Mr. Kaplan," frowned Mr. Parkhill, "you are disturbing the class."

"I back you podden." The injured air signified that Mr. Kaplan could not think clearly if forbidden to whisper to himself.

" 'Heat' . . ." Mr. Parkhill wished Mr. Kaplan would not look as if he were David robbed of his slingshot. " 'Heat.' "

" 'Heat,' " Mr. Kaplan automatically echoed, then caught himself; he pressed his lips together and, in melancholy mufflement, wrote a sentence using "heat."

" 'Pack' . . . 'excite' . . . 'throat.' "

Mr. Parkhill announced each word slowly, allowing a

174

full minute to elapse before he uttered the next syllables; and he articulated each word with the utmost precision. ("Excite" he repeated three times.)

So well did Mr. Parkhill time his recitation that he called the last of the thirty test words a good forty seconds before the recess bell tinkled. He waited for a few laggards to complete a sentence using "Adorable."

"The first part of our examination is over," he declared. "Please hand in your papers."

Relief swept the beleaguered ranks. Students rose, stretched, rubbed their temples, massaged their fingers, handed in their pages and ambled into the corridor—to share and compare, describe and debate the sentences they had manufactured. Their voices were very loud, and Mr. Nathan was playing "Yes, Sir, That's My Baby" in the lower register of his harmonica.

Mr. Parkhill began to scan the papers. Miss Mitnick had, as usual, done excellently. Mrs. Yanoff seemed to have struck disaster with "throat," for she had written several sentences, scratched them out, and in panic settled for "He throat the ball." Mr. Parkhill came to the paper headed H*Y*M*A*N  K*A*P*L*A*N:

1. My brother's girl is my *neece* and has two *neez*.
2. I *heat* him on the head, the big fool.
3. When we buy potatos we buy potatos by the *pack*.
4. In theatres is the insite, the outsite, and the *exite* (in case Fire).

Mr. Parkhill read no further.

At 8:40 the bell clanged an end to recess; the victims rumbled in for the completion of their ordeal. Some looked worried, some confident, some tense. Miss Mitnick looked happy, for Nathan P. Nathan was holding her hand. Mrs. Moskowitz and Mr. Kaplan entered side by side. Common adversity had oiled the waters of their enmity. Mrs. Moskowitz was moaning, "I'm *sha*king, Mr. Keplan."

Mr. Kaplan waved with aplomb. *"Stop* de shakink. Kip high your had! Dis pot vill be a *snep!"*

The dolorous matron sighed. "I wish I had your noives."

Mr. Kaplan graciously inclined his head. "If you fill blue, remamber det vunderful song: 'Heppy Dace Is Here Vunce More!' " As Mr. Kaplan sat down, he tossed a final bone of encouragement across the tiers: "Moskovitz, don't give op de sheep!"

Mr. Parkhill tapped the desk sharply. "Well, class . . . the second part of our examination will be a one-page essay— on any topic you wish!"

The falling of faces advertised to the quicksand of the assignment.

"A whole paitch?" gasped Bessie Shimmelfarb.

*"Any* topic?" quavered Mr. Scymczak.

Mr. Kaplan rallied the faint of heart. "I like any sobjeck!"

"Keplan . . ." moaned Mrs. Moskowitz, in an S.O.S.

Mr. Parkhill cleared his throat. "I must request that you do *not* talk to each other." He looked squarely at the knight in the center of the front row. "No prompting, please, to *or* from another student!"

Mr. Kaplan winced. Mrs. Moskowitz looked as if her arm had been cut off.

"Class, you will have ample time to reread your one-page compositions carefully, as I trust you will, to correct errors in spelling, to watch your capital letters, to rewrite. . . ." He strolled down the aisle.

The silence of concentration swathed the beginners' grade as its constituents searched for topics within the compass of their capability. Miss Caravello stared at the picture of Lincoln on the wall, seeking first-aid from that compassionate countenance. Mr. Finsterwald muttered a cryptic appeal to austere Washington. "Cookie" Kipnis pressed her fists against her temples to intensify her concentration. Mr. Trabish was either cogitating or napping (since he was not snoring, it was hard to tell). The Misses Valuskas and Mitnick had long since begun writing. Mr. Nathan was charting an out-of-bounds stratagem before committing it to prose.

Soon the congregation was scribbling away: Mr. Perez breathing Iberian cues, Mr. Schmitt hissing Germanic props, Miss Goldberg consuming one jellybean after another to stoke the furnace of cerebration.

Mr. Parkhill stopped next to Mrs. Moskowitz, who was fanning her cheeks with her notebook.

"Is anything wrong?" he whispered.

Mrs. Moskowitz raised a haggard face. "I ken't t'ink of a sobject!"

"Well—er—why not try 'My Ambition'?" ("My Ambition" had always proved *very* popular.)

Mrs. Moskowitz went limp. "Who has embition?! I have hot flashes."

"Then—how about 'My First Day in America'?"

"My foist day I broke my wrisk."

Mr. Parkhill felt miserable. "Er—then suppose—"

A whistling wafted through the air, its refrain unmistakable: "Heppy Dace Is Here Vunce More."

"Mr. Kap—"

The whistling stopped; but it was replaced by disembodied whispers: " 'Should Ladies Smoke?' . . . 'Is Dere a God, Ectual?' . . ."

"Mr. Kaplan!"

But the subversive communication had been consummated.

"I'll write about a *qvastion!*" croaked Mrs. Moskowitz.

Mr. Parkhill moved on.

"Podden me, Mr. Pockheel."

Firmly, Mr. Parkhill shook his head. "No question."

177

"Is no qvastion," said Mr. Kaplan. "De room is too varm. Should I aupen a vindow?"

"Oh."

Mr. Kaplan rose, "aupened" a window, and returned to his chair. At once, Miss Gidwitz, on his left, put her mouth close to his ear.

"No whispering, please . . ."

Mr. Kaplan stood up again. "I batter close de vindow. Is on Gidvitz a cold graft."

He had lowered the window before Mr. Parkhill could say, " 'Draft,' Mr. Kaplan, 'draft.' "

Mr. Parkhill felt relieved, yet a bit sad, when the terminal bell—the last angelus of the season—chimed. (Only once, in all her years at the American Night Preparatory School for Adults, had Miss Schnepfe not pressed the bell button in the principal's office exactly on time. *That* night, classes had continued a full eight minutes after 10 P.M., because a mouse had scurried around Miss Schnepfe's office. The guardian of the bells jumped up on her chair and shrieked like a banshee. Fortunately, Mr. Robinson entered, took in the crisis at a glance, chased the mouse out by waving his hat and crying "Whoosh! Whoosh!," and pressed the button himself. . . . How Mr. Krout had regaled the faculty, the next night, remarking that Mr. Robinson was a wizard when it came to smelling a rat!)

The ringing pring rolled down the corridor. The beginners' grade collected their artifacts. They crowded up to Mr. Parkhill's desk to hand in their papers and bid him adieu. They behaved like any class in any school whenever a semester ends: some cheerful, some wistful, some grieving the cessation of learning, some welcoming the free nights ahead. Each pupil shook Mr. Parkhill's hand; each bade him farewell.

"Good-bye and good luck in anything that should happen to you!" was Mr. Bloom's hearty adieu.

Miss Mitnick curtseyed. "Every lesson was a real pleasure!" Her cheeks turned as pink as petunias. "I learned so much. I want to come back."

"Perhaps you'll be with Miss Higby in the fall," smiled Mr. Parkhill.

"I don't *want* to change teachers!" bleated Miss Mitnick, and fled.

"Me, too!" laughed Mr. Nathan.

Mr. Scymczak ran a hand across his crew-cut and blurted hoarsely, "You teach good, good. Thanks."

"Thank you, Mr. Scymczak."

Miss Caravello simply sang out, *"Arrivederci!"* and soared off on wings of deliverance.

Mr. Matsoukas's syllables of departure were not more comprehensible than his habitual mumbles.

Mr. Pinsky chuckled, "Another sizzon! Work findished! Thank you. *Shalom!"*

Miss Ziev's swan song smothered in a fit of coughing.

Throughout these fervent valedictories, Hyman Kaplan hovered on the edges of the throng proudly. He might have been Mr. Parkhill's mentor, savoring the praises to his protégé.

Olga Tarnova took Mr. Parkhill's hand in both of hers, jangling her bracelets, as she crooned, "Thonk you, thonk you. In Rossian we say, *'Sposibo, sposibo.'* "She bent so low that Mr. Parkhill feared she was about to kiss his knuckles; then she crouched. Mr. Parkhill, alarmed that she would kiss his shoes, exclaimed, "Miss Tar—!" but it turned out that Miss Tarnova had merely dropped her scented handkerchief, which, recovered, waved a gaudy exit.

Mrs. Rodriguez said, "I don't theenk I come back—"

"I hope you will," said Mr. Parkhill.

"Thees means I *failed?!"* cried Mrs. Rodriguez.

"Oh, no. I just meant I hope you'll return to—"

*"That* means I failed!"

"No, no—"

"Rodriguez!" cut in Mr. Kaplan. "Pull yourself altogadder!"

Wolfgang Schmitt had marched up, stiffened, and declaimed: "Not in all my time in Chermany, I did haff zuch exzellent teaching!"

"In Joiminy, they shouldn't say 'Chermany,'" observed Mr. Kaplan.

And so it went: Miss Goldberg wiping her fingers of chocolate before shaking her master's hand ("A *mil*lion thenks!"), Vincente Perez blurting a mystifying, "My house ees your house!," Mrs. Moskowitz, liberated from bondage, burbling moist incoherences.

Now they were all gone—all save Hyman Kaplan, who approached the desk.

Mr. Parkhill adjusted his glasses. *"Well,* Mr. Kaplan . . ."

Mr. Kaplan shook hands. He turned to cast one last, fond glance across the empty tiers, around the blackboards, over the whole jousting ground on which so many battles had raged: Kaplan versus Mitnick, Kaplan versus Bloom, the Kaplan-Pinsky-Trabish phalanx breaching the Blattberg-Tarnova-Caravello flanks. . . . "Soch good times ve had in dis room!" sighed the warrior. He shook off reverie and strode to the door—from which he waved as if he (Mr. Kaplan) was on a ship and he (Mr. Parkhill) was seeing him off on a historic voyage. "Don't vorry," said Mr. Kaplan. He passed through the portal.

Mr. Parkhill wondered what on earth made Mr. Kaplan say a thing like that. He began to fill his briefcase: the class records, the students' exam papers. He riffled them out of curiosity. The titles fluttered before him: "The Stateu of Liberty," "A Sad Night in Hospital," "Should be a Panelty

for Murdering?" (That was surely Mr. Kaplan's offering—
no, it was Mrs. Moskowitz's; but it certainly owed all to Mr.
Kaplan's advice.)

Mr. Parkhill stuffed the lot into his case and picked
up the remaining batch: "My Children Make Me a
Happy Life," "How We Beat the Manischewitz Rockets,"
"I Like Ice Cream!," "Thinking About." He winced. He
read the title again: "Thinking About." Mr. Parkhill
could not prevent himself from raising that sheet above
the rest.

"THINKING ABOUT"
*(Humans & Animals)*
by
H*Y*M*A*N   K*A*P*L*A*N


*1.*

Sometime I feel sad about how people are living. Only
eating, working, sleeping. No *thinking!*

(Mr. Kaplan's spelling certainly had improved.)

These people are like enimals the same, which don't use
one pot of their brans. Humans should not be like enimals.

(Mr. Parkhill modified his opinion of Mr. Kaplan's spelling.)

Now we are having the good-bye exemination. Mostly
will the class write a story. But I ask, Why must allways be
a story? Mr. P. must be sick and tied up from reading storys,
storys, storys.

Kaplan, *Be a man!* No story. Tell better about *thinking*
something. Fine. Now I am thinking.

(Mr. Parkhill sank into the chair.)

In resess, some students asked if is right to say "Its Me"
or "Its I" (because maybe we will have that question *after*
resess.) "Its Me" or "Its I?" A very hard question, no? Yes.

But it isnt so hard if we *think about!*

I figgure this way: If sombody is in the hall and makes
knok, knok, knok on my door—I holler, netcheral, "Whose
there"?

Comes the answer "Its me."

Som answer! Rotten!! Who is that Me anyho? Can I tell?
No! So is "Its Me" a bad way to anser "Who is it?"

Again is knok, knok, knok. Again I holler "Whose there"?
Now comes the answer "Its I."

Is that an anser?! Crazy! Who is that I?? Can I (Kaplan)
tell?? Ha! Umpossible!

So is "Its I" also no-good, an anser that isnt an *anser!*

So it looks like their *is no good anser!* But—(Turn around
paige)

As Mr. Parkhill turned the page "around" (Mr. Kaplan had
interpreted "a one-page essay" with characteristic
generosity) he reflected that put that way, the puzzle of
"It's Me" or "It's I" was practically a Gordian knot.

But must be *som kind good anser!* So how can we find
it??? BY THINKING ABOUT.

(Now comes how Humans are more smart then Enimals!)

If *I* am in the hall and make knok, knok, knok, and I hear
from insite (insite the room) sombody hollers "Whose
there"?—*I* anser, "Hyman Kaplan!"

Aha! Now is plain, clear like gold. No chance *enyone* in U.S. will mix up a Me, I, You, Who? Ect.

This shows how by *thinking* Humans are making big advences on enimals.

This I call Progriss.

T-H-E  E-N-D

A postscript climaxed this dazzling demonstration of pure reason:

*To Mr. P.*

ps.

I dont care if I dont pass. I just *love* the class.

# FOR THE BEST IN PAPERBACKS, LOOK FOR THE

In every corner of the world, on every subject under the sun, Penguin represents quality and variety – the very best in publishing today.

For complete information about books available from Penguin – including Pelicans, Puffins, Peregrines and Penguin Classics – and how to order them, write to us at the appropriate address below. Please note that for copyright reasons the selection of books varies from country to country.

---

**In the United Kingdom:** For a complete list of books available from Penguin in the U.K., please write to *Dept E.P., Penguin Books Ltd, Harmondsworth, Middlesex, UB7 0DA*

**In the United States:** For a complete list of books available from Penguin in the U.S., please write to *Dept BA, Penguin, 299 Murray Hill Parkway, East Rutherford, New Jersey 07073*

**In Canada:** For a complete list of books available from Penguin in Canada, please write to *Penguin Books Canada Ltd, 2801 John Street, Markham, Ontario L3R 1B4*

**In Australia:** For a complete list of books available from Penguin in Australia, please write to the *Marketing Department, Penguin Books Australia Ltd, P.O. Box 257, Ringwood, Victoria 3134*

**In New Zealand:** For a complete list of books available from Penguin in New Zealand, please write to the *Marketing Department, Penguin Books (NZ) Ltd, Private Bag, Takapuna, Auckland 9*

**In India:** For a complete list of books available from Penguin, please write to *Penguin Overseas Ltd, 706 Eros Apartments, 56 Nehru Place, New Delhi, 110019*

**In Holland:** For a complete list of books available from Penguin in Holland, please write to *Penguin Books Nederland B.V., Postbus 195, NL–1380AD Weesp, Netherlands*

**In Germany:** For a complete list of books available from Penguin, please write to *Penguin Books Ltd, Friedrichstrasse 10 – 12, D–6000 Frankfurt Main 1, Federal Republic of Germany*

**In Spain:** For a complete list of books available from Penguin in Spain, please write to *Longman Penguin España, Calle San Nicolas 15, E–28013 Madrid, Spain*

### Life with Jeeves   P. G. Wodehouse

Containing *Right Ho, Jeeves*, *The Inimitable Jeeves* and *Very Good, Jeeves!*, this is a delicious collection of vintage Wodehouse in which the old master lures us, once again, into the evergreen world of Bertie Wooster, his terrifying Aunt Agatha, and, of course, the inimitable Jeeves.

### Perfick! Perfick!   H. E. Bates

The adventures of the irrepressible Larkin family, in four novels: *The Darling Buds of May*, *A Breath of French Air*, *When the Green Woods Laugh* and *Oh! To Be in England*.

### The Best of Modern Humour   Edited by Mordecai Richler

Packed between the covers of this book is the teeming genius of modern humour's foremost exponents from both sides of the Atlantic – and for every conceivable taste. Here is everyone from Tom Wolfe, S. J. Perelman, John Mortimer, Alan Coren, Woody Allen, John Berger and Fran Lebowitz to P. G. Wodehouse, James Thurber and Evelyn Waugh.

### Enderby   Anthony Burgess

'These three novels are the richest and most verbally dazzling comedies Burgess has written' – *Listener*. Containing the three volumes *Inside Enderby*, *Enderby Outside* and *The Clockwork Treatment*.

### Vintage Thurber: Vol. One   James Thurber

A selection of his best writings and drawings, this *grand-cru* volume includes *Let Your Mind Alone*, *My World and Welcome to It*, *Fables for Our Time*, *Famous Poems Illustrated*, *Men, Women and Dogs*, *The Beast in Me* and *Thurber Country* – as well as much, much more.

### Vintage Thurber: Vol. Two   James Thurber

'Without question America's foremost humorist' – *The Times Literary Supplement*. In this volume, where vintage piles upon vintage, are *The Middle-aged Man on the Flying Trapeze*, *The Last Flower*, *My Life and Hard Times*, *The Owl in the Attic*, *The Seal in the Bedroom* and *The Thurber Carnival*.